COWGIRL FALLIN' FOR HER BEST FRIEND'S BROTHER

BRIDES OF MILLER RANCH, N.M. BOOK 5

NATALIE DEAN

DEDICATION

I'd like to dedicate this book to YOU! The readers of my books. Without your interest in reading these heartwarming stories of love, I wouldn't have made it this far. So thank you so much for taking the time to read any and hopefully all of my books.

And I can't leave out my wonderful mother, son, sister, and Auntie. I love you all, and thank you for helping me make this happen.

Most of all, I thank God for blessing me on this endeavor.

AND... I've got a special team of advance readers who are always so helpful in pointing out any last minute corrections that need to be made. I'm so thankful to those of you who are so helpful!

OTHER BOOKS BY NATALIE DEAN

CONTEMPORARY ROMANCE

Miller Family Saga

BROTHERS OF MILLER RANCH

Miller Family Saga Series 1

Her Second Chance Cowboy

Saving Her Cowboy

Her Rival Cowboy

Her Fake-Fiance Cowboy Protector

Taming Her Cowboy Billionaire

Brothers of Miller Ranch Complete Collection

MILLER BROTHERS OF TEXAS

Miller Family Saga Series 2

The New Cowboy at Miller Ranch Prologue

Humbling Her Cowboy

In Debt to the Cowboy

The Cowboy Falls for the Veterinarian

Almost Fired by the Cowboy

Faking a Date with Her Cowboy Boss

Miller Brothers of Texas Complete Collection

BRIDES OF MILLER RANCH, N.M.

Miller Family Saga Series 3

Cowgirl Fallin' for the Single Dad

Cowgirl Fallin' for the Ranch Hand

Cowgirl Fallin' for the Neighbor

Cowgirl Fallin' for the Miller Brother

Cowgirl Fallin' for Her Best Friend's Brother

Cowboy Fallin' in Love Again

Brides of Miller Ranch Complete Collection

Miller Family Wrap-up Story

(An update on all your favorite characters!)

Copper Creek Romances

BAKER BROTHERS OF COPPER CREEK

Copper Creek Romances Series 1

Cowboys & Protective Ways

Cowboys & Crushes

Cowboys & Christmas Kisses

Cowboys & Broken Hearts

Cowboys & Second Chances

Cowboys & Wedding Woes

Cowboys' Mom Finds Love

Baker Brothers of Copper Creek Complete Collection

CALLAHANS OF COPPER CREEK

Copper Creek Romances Series 2

Making a Cowgirl

Marrying a Cowgirl

Christmas with a Cowgirl

Trusting a Cowgirl

Dating a Cowgirl

Catching a Cowgirl

Loving a Cowgirl

Marrying a Cowboy

Callahans of Copper Creek Complete Collection

KEAGANS OF COPPER CREEK

Copper Creek Romances Series 3

Some Cowboys are Off-Limits

Some Cowgirls Love Single Dads

Some Cowboys are Infuriating

Some Cowboys Don't Like City Girls

Some Cowboys Heal Broken Hearts

Some Cowgirls are Worth Protecting

Some Cowboys are Just Friends (Coming August 2024)

Though I try to keep this list updated in each book, you may also visit my website nataliedeanauthor.com for the most up to date information on my book list.

CONTENTS

1

Cecilia

"Uh, Clara, I think I jammed the machine again," Cici said, brow furrowed as she looked at the jumble of thread hanging from the hem she was working on. If she hadn't already had to seam-rip two other similar spots, she would be worried that she'd ruined Sabra's wedding gift.

"Are you sure? It didn't sound like it from over here."

Clara got up from where she was drafting a pattern on some sort of fancy design program on her computer and crossed to Cici, moving aside the gossamer-like fabric to look at the sewing machine.

"Oh! It looks like your bobbin just ran out and you sewed for a while on it so the top thread just got a little tangled. You don't have to worry."

"The bobbin? That's the bottom thread, right?"

Clara practically beamed. "You remembered! Do you know how to fill it again? I have pre-filled ones, but it's good for you to get the practice while you're here."

"Now that's something I can get on board with."

Clara patiently walked Cici through how to fill the little ring and put it back into the machine. Cici had been sewing for about roughly a month, and she had only just begun working on the whole reason she'd picked up the hobby.

Which was a beautiful, ethereal sort of dressing gown for her best friend who wasn't actually related to her, Sabra Gamal. Her wedding was coming up in the fall and Cici had roughly nine or so months to finish the thing.

And she was going to need all of those months, because although the pattern was simple (according to Clara) it was truly a voluminous garment fit for a princess.

A soft white with ivory trim, it was definitely an undertaking, but the real kicker was all the hand embroidery Cici planned on adding to the bottom and the binding of the trim. While she hadn't been sewing long, she'd always loved needlepoint and figured she might as well use the skill that she'd started because she saw Sabra doing it all the way back in second grade.

"Good job! I can't believe how quickly you're picking this up! It's so nice to have one of you sew with me."

"It helps that it's winter," Cici said with a grin, feeling validated. Maybe from someone else, Clara's praise would sound infantilizing, but Cici knew her sister well enough to tell that her excitement was genuine. No one loved fashion and sewing as much as Clara and it had to be pretty awesome to have someone to share it with. "Less chores lets me focus."

"That's true. You have been a wonderful sort of catch-all ever since you came back, my little graduate."

"Who you calling little?" Cici retorted in their stereotypical banter. "Just because I'm not a six-foot amazon doesn't mean I'm *little*."

"You keep telling yourself that."

Cici responded by throwing an empty spool of thread at her sister, and Clara let out a loud, peeling laugh. Ahhh, Cici had missed goofing off with her siblings. She'd loved college and she was glad that she'd completed her degree, but there really wasn't anything like home.

"Remember, you want to add the appliques to the sleeves and the front before you start gathering. Your hand embroidery will be fine, but trying to do it once the whole garment is assembled will be about three times as difficult."

"I remember, but thank you for reminding me. I want this to be perfect for Sabra."

"You two really are platonic soulmates, aren't you?"

"BFFs for life, as the kids are saying these days."

"Clara, you're twenty-four. You are a kid."

"Now you sound like Charity."

"I take that as a compliment," Clara said with faux haughtiness, her nose in the air. That lasted about a minute before they both broke into chuckles. "Alright, I'm going to make tea. Would you like some?"

"Oooh, the peach kind?"

"I'm feeling more like hibiscus today."

Cici wavered a moment before giving her taller sister a look through her lashes. "Could you maybe do... hibiscus *with* peach?"

Another sweet laugh from her and Clara ruffled Cici's hair. The youngest Miller batted her sibling's hand away, sending her a mock-glare. "Alright, I can do that. I'll be back in fifteen."

Cici nodded and went back to her work. Although she was a bit intimidated by her project, she was incredibly excited for it.

Sabra had been her best friend since kindergarten and they'd been thick as thieves. She was there through everything, including the death of Cici's mother and her health derailment after that.

Cici grimaced, something she couldn't help considering how awful thinking back on that time was. Between the panic attacks, the night terrors, the survivor's guilt and the guilt of causing so much trouble for her family, it had been a rough couple of years. But thanks to Papa getting her into therapy, her entire family supporting her, and even Sabra and her own folks helping, Cici had gotten to the other side.

She owed them everything.

And sure, she had plenty of money. She could buy a hundred or so expensive, designer dressing gowns until Sabra was drowning in them. But Cici wanted to do more than that. She wanted something that spoke to just how much Sabra meant to her.

So, she figured learning an entirely new skill and making something by hand was the best way to do that.

Sabra was going to be *so* surprised.

Granted, that was mostly because Papa was maybe-kinda-sorta-absolutely paying for all of Sabra's wedding because Cici had asked him to.

It was never anything she'd planned on. At first, Sabra's wedding was going to be a simple church affair with maybe ten guests and a backyard reception. Not that there was anything wrong with that, there wasn't. But then Cici had learned that Sabra had always dreamed of a more lavish, nature mixed with fantasy wedding and she *had* to give her friend the perfect wedding.

After all, Cici was pretty sure that she wouldn't have gotten through college without Sabra either. Even though they'd been accepted into different schools, they'd kept in contact and had weekly video chats along with phone calls about every other day. She was Cici's rock away from home and deserved *so* much.

"Hey there, sugar, ya busy?"

Cici practically jumped and looked to the door where none other than Ms. Daisy Dixon was standing. It was certainly unusual to have her brother's girlfriend living on the ranch with them, but after hearing her story, Cici was glad she had a safe, supportive place to stay.

And it wasn't like the woman didn't work to earn her keep.

"I'm just working on this and waiting for Clara to finish up some tea."

"Oooh, is it that yummy peach tea of hers?"

"Peach-hibiscus, actually."

"Wow, sounds fancy."

Cici smiled, giving a nod. She liked Daisy's enthusiasm for everything and her blunt way of talking. Her saying the tea was fancy wasn't an insult, just an appreciation for all the work Clara put into the herbal blends.

"You think she'd be alright if I got a little bit of it?"

"Knowing Clara, I think she'd be insulted if you didn't want some."

"Hah! Ain't that right. Between her and your brother, I'm gonna get all soft." Daisy rubbed her stomach, which admittedly had gotten much less gaunt since she'd moved onto the Miller Ranch. "But hey, once teatime is done, would you be willing to teach me about the warmer weather seedlings coming up? Clara said she'd take me to her Nathan fella's to help, but I don't want to go there like a total numpty."

"Yeah, sure! I'd be happy to help you with that."

"Really? Thanks! I'm not gonna lie, I like your fall garden and the early weather brassicas, but I'm *real* excited for the spring garden."

"You and Papa both. If you want to hang around here, Clara should be back soon."

"Sounds good! Maybe I'll even be able to leave without Clara foisting another costume onto me."

"Doubt that."

They both shared a laugh, knowing that Clara had really taken to dressing Daisy up as her own personal rodeo doll and would look for any excuse to make another ensemble. Warmth bubbled up in Cici as she thought of the last fitting Daisy had been in, protesting that the baby blue number was far too beautiful and expensive while Clara just hummed along agreeably.

It was nice to be a part of the ranch again, to be surrounded by the interconnected lives of her siblings. It was familiar and warm, but also enhanced, with Mickey, Daisy, Alejandro, Nathan and Savannah adding to it.

Oh, and that cute librarian that Papa was trying to pretend he wasn't dating. Couldn't forget her.

Smiling to herself, Cici returned to her work yet again until Clara returned. From there, she carefully packed her entire project up so that none of the ruby-red tea could accidentally get anywhere near it. Then she enjoyed about an hour chatting with the other two women.

Once that was done, she and Daisy headed outside to the greenhouse that Charity had built as a birthday gift for Papa just a few months earlier. Cici wasn't sure why they'd never had one, but Papa was absolutely thrilled.

"Ya know, sometimes when I walk in here, I feel like I'm walking into a different world," Daisy remarked, looking around with a wonderous grin. That was another thing that Cici liked about the rodeo star; she was a romantic at heart, just like Cici.

"I know what you mean. Like Middle Earth or Narnia or something."

"Yeah! You know, I've been meaning to read Lord of the Rings again. Haven't in at least four years."

"You like Lord of the Rings?"

"Who doesn't?"

"Most people, in my experience. Especially when you're not talking about the movies."

"Aw, fair point. But they don't know what-"

Her words were cut off as a loud, unfamiliar honk sounded from the front of the house.

"What in the Good Lord's name is that?"

"I dunno," Cici said, eyes wide. "Let's go see."

For someone who used to be plagued with panic attacks, Cici sure didn't have a problem delving into the unknown. She rushed around the house, with no idea what car that horn belonged to and with no worries about any potential danger or surprise.

Another honk as she rounded the corner and she realized it was a massive delivery truck of construction supplies.

"Ah, that must be for Charity's house," she said as Daisy caught up with her.

"Wow, you're speedy. And oh yeah, I forgot about that. So that's why your sister's been scarce around here. Just figured she was in town."

"No, just busy building the home of her dreams."

"Crazy that she's doing that by herself."

"Well, she's got Cass, Charlie, and my cousin Benji from up north."

"*Riiight,* I remember that. His wife is the big lady with the two kids who sing all the time."

Cici gave Daisy a sharp look at her description of Dani, but it was clear that the rodeo rider didn't mean any insult by it. Cici used to be a lot more protective of her plus-sized cousin-in-law until Dani took her aside and said there's nothing inherently wrong with words like 'fat', 'big' 'plus-sized' or other simple adjectives. It was how people used them, how they put poisonous tone or prejudices in them that could make those words cruel.

"All three of them do have lovely voices, don't they?" Cici said instead.

"Yup. Can't say the same for myself. I sound like a bundle of cats in a bag with some nickels thrown in for good measure."

"Charlie says he loves to hear you sing."

"Charlie is a blind fool in love, and I adore that about him."

Cici couldn't help but snort-laugh at that. Because it was true. Charlie was so clearly smitten by his love that everyone could see it. It was lovely, really, especially since he'd confided in what had happened when he'd went to college and why he'd suddenly dropped out.

Cici felt terrible for her brother, she did, but whenever she saw the love that he and Daisy shared, it made her heart glow. And they weren't alone. She saw how sometimes Alejandro would rub Charity's feet after a long day, or how he'd cook her things when she visited so she didn't have to make anything herself. She even saw Mr. Westbrook more often, the reclusive man pushing himself to visit more and more as a show of effort for Clara. And then there were Mickey and Cass, who were borderline inseparable a majority of the time and had created an entirely new exercise and training regimen for their horses.

It was wonderful, really, seeing her family grow and multiply with happiness. But somewhere hidden in her compersion was the mournful wondering if her heart would ever be able to move on so she could have the same thing her siblings did.

2

—————

Baz

Baz lowered his music as he pulled up to his parent's house, making sure to leave plenty of space between their old, secondhand minivan and his completely restored Mercedes SL 300 Gullwing. He'd put two full years of work into it and that was plenty of time to learn that he needed a wider span to raise the doors.

As soon as he took his keys out of the ignition, the front door slammed open, and an excited scream sounded from the entrance. Chuckling, he got out, only for his sister to slam into him with a pretty considerable force for her small frame.

"Glad to see you too, Sabra," he said with a chuckle, hugging her back.

"Ugh, it's been *forever,* you jerk! I missed you!"

"Makes sense. I'm pretty amazing."

"You totally stole that line from something and I don't even care because I'm so happy to see you."

Baz softened, giving her an extra squeeze. "I missed you too."

He was well aware that many people were surprised by how close he and his sister were, seeing as how most siblings around town went about their own paths once they hit adulthood, but they'd gone through a lot together. It was a special bond, being first generation Americans and helping teach their parents English and watching their family build itself from the ground up. And even though she could be annoying—as all little sisters were—he loved her deeply.

"Sabra, stop hugging your brother and let me strangle him!"

"You mean smother him, *waleda*, like smothering him with affection."

"Oy, you knew what I meant."

Baz let go of his sister only to go to his mother, whose arms were already outstretched where she stood on the porch. It was funny how she could stand on the top step and he could be on the ground but still be taller than her, and it struck him just how little she was. When he was a kid, she'd been an unstoppable giant. Working as a cleaner for several families in town, learning English, going to night classes in the city and raising her family, her and Dad had done it all.

"Hello, son. It is good to see you again."

As if on cue, the low rumble of his father came from the doorway. Still hugging his mother, Baz gave the patriarch of the family a nod.

"It's good to be seen. I missed all of you. I missed *home*."

"Well, you're here now, so there's no reason to miss anything," Sabra said, bounding up behind them. Sometimes it was easy to forget that she was twenty-five years old; she still so often had the energy of a particularly caffeinated teenager. "Come in! We made you cake!"

Baz happily followed them in, feeling more comfortable than he had in a while. It was like he'd been walking around on tacks but hadn't realized it until just then and the relief was heady.

Why had he even left? Home was like a warm, comfortable blanket that a lot of people never got to enjoy. It was a place with hugs and cake and good meals and silly arguments. A place of love.

Oh, right. He'd had a chance to be part of the opening crew for a vintage motor shop in the city and he'd jumped on the amazing opportunity. And it worked out well for him, with his pay doubling while he got to do something he loved.

But then a smaller voice reminded him that one of the main reasons was because of *her*.

Ugh. That was definitely a mistake.

"And since you just got home, I'll let you get first dibs on which slice you want," Sabra said, flicking on the small kitchen's light.

"How magnanimous of you."

"Of course. I am nothing if not benevolent."

She gave a dramatic bow and it was hard to believe that she was all grown up and getting married! She was just a quarter of a century and two years younger than him, but she'd been dating the same guy since senior year of high school.

And he was a good guy too, as far as Baz could tell. Cameron Abolos was a local and son of the grocery store owner. He was a nerdy fellow, into math and computers, but that suited fantastical Sabra just fine.

That was one thing about his little sister he'd always worried about. She was endlessly creative but with her head so high in the clouds he was sometimes worried she wouldn't notice a threat headed towards her on the ground until it was too late. It didn't help that her best friend in the world was equally as starry eyed and fantastical.

Or, in other words, absolute nerds.

"Sabra, you've spent too much time being spoiled by the Millers. Dinner before cake," their mother said, clicking her tongue in that way of hers that was far too full of affection for such a simple sound.

"But it's a special occasion. It's not every day my brother comes home to stay for a while." There was a slight waver to her happy expression. "You are staying for a bit, right?"

Baz knew it was time to assure her and he sent her the most beaming grin that he could. "I wouldn't miss this time for the world."

His sister practically melted into a grin. It was sappy, sure, but Baz didn't mind. His sister wore her heart on her sleeve and he'd always admired that about her. He wished he could say the same, but with everything that had happened lately, he felt... guarded.

No, that wasn't the right word.

Weary.

That was more like it. Like the weight of the world was pressing against him, dragging him deeper and deeper into the muck until he was stuck in the mud and mire of it all. He just wanted to go back to being relatively carefree and limitless, back when anything was possible and their dreams were everything.

That time seemed so long ago. Almost another lifetime. He wasn't sure when he'd lost that spark, that daringness to dream and dream big, but it was somewhere far beyond his reach.

But not Sabra's.

"Come, sit, sit, I already have the food waiting in the oven."

"Yes, I've been forced to smell it all day," their father added. "It has been pure torture, but you are worth it."

"I'm already here, you don't have to keep buttering me up."

"Maybe you could use some more butter. You are too skinny, living in the city all alone!"

"*Mom*," Sabra cut in. "Don't badger him right when he gets in the door! You'll chase him off again!"

But the matriarch just scoffed and switched to Arabic. "*Please, I raised your brother too well for that. He would never miss the wedding of his baby sister.*"

"*That's right,*" Baz agreed. "*I didn't put in all those big brother hours not to embarrass you at your own reception.*"

"Don't you dare!" Sabra shouted back in English. She could speak their native language alright, but she used it the least of any of in the family.

"*Try and stop me.*"

"That's it. We duel at-"

"*You duel after dinner. For now, sit down.*"

They did exactly that and it was just like old times, sitting around their small kitchen table and eating delicious food. They caught up on so much and every so often Sabra would tell him a new duty that he had for her wedding. Although he was nervous about his position and a little melancholy about his sister going off to start her own family, he was overall very excited for her. If anyone deserved a happily ever after, it was Sabra.

Because it certainly wasn't going to be him.

"So, I'm going to need you to either give me your measurements or go to Cici's and have her sister take them."

"Cici?" he repeated, his mind flooding with so many memories of babysitting his little sister and her best friend. "How is that lil' pipsqueak doing?"

"Oh, that's right, you haven't seen her since she went off to college."

Baz nodded. "Only heard her occasionally when you were on the phone while visiting me a couple times."

"Well, she's doing great. She decided to grow her hair out. It's super long now."

"What, really?" Baz vaguely remembered that the girl had always worn her hair in two long braids up until her mother died. Although Papa Miller had clearly tried his best after his wife passed, and Charity definitely stepped up to help, there were only so many hands to go around and little Cecilia's hair ended up matted and tangled more often than not. That resulted in the little girl taking a pair of scissors to her head and she'd kept it in either a short bob or pixie cut ever since. And the only reason Baz even knew the names of those hairstyles was because Sabra insisted on wearing her hair the exact same way until their junior year of high school.

"Yup. And it's already longer than mine. It's not fair, I tell you."

"*You should take those vitamins your mother got you.*"

"Those were pregnancy vitamins. I don't need them, Dad."

"Not yet at least," Baz added.

"*I just want you to be healthy and prepared for when it's time to give us grandchildren.*"

"Mother!" Finally, Sabra switched to Arabic. "*That is not dinner table talk.*"

"*No, it is lonely grandmother talk. Both my babies are grown, I need new ones to spoil!*"

"Oh boy..."

The conversation went from there, switching every which way and being playfully dramatic several times. By the time it ended and cake was devoured, at least a couple of hours had passed.

Baz cleaned up in the familiar bathroom that he hadn't been in in ages, then headed to his room. Part of the small space had been turned into a painting area by his father, but Baz's bed was still there as well as his various awards that dotted the wall. He stopped to look at the art his father had been working on and grinned.

He'd never inherited the art gene, but that didn't mean he didn't appreciate his father's skill. If he had his way, his father would have some of his works in a museum for everyone to enjoy.

Too bad Baz rarely got his way. Especially when it came to love.

Sighing at his brain for taking it in that direction, he flopped into his bed and let himself drift off.

Home was where the heart was, right? But where exactly was that when his heart was smashed to dust months ago?

3

———

Cecilia

"Okay, so I've been doing some research and I've decided that I want to have a dry wedding."

"Really?" Cici asked, setting her lemonade down. "What prompted that?"

"Well, when our wedding was just supposed to be about ten or so people, I knew I could trust everyone to behave themselves. But, since there's almost a hundred now, there's always bound to be a couple of people who ruin things for everyone. I'd rather have sparkling apple juice, sparkling grape juice, and mock cocktails than have to deal with any mess."

"You know what, I see where you're coming from, and mocktails are yummy as it is."

Cici didn't have anything against people drinking, and if she ever married, she might have champagne at her wedding. But all in all, she did think that too many events revolved around alcohol and society was borderline obsessed with it in some ways.

Granted, her feelings towards libations had shifted greatly since finding out about Charlie's college experience and even Daisy's struggle. There was a reason that there wasn't any alcohol set out in the house anymore and Cici didn't miss it.

"Exactly! Who doesn't love a good mocktail. Oh, and also, I'm thinking of like... a tea bar? Or a barista to make specialty coffees? It was one of the suggestions on the list your Papa gave me."

"Right, the list that *Papa* gave you."

Sabra recognized Cici's tone instantly and narrowed her eyes at the Miller. "Cecilia Miller, did you write this list?"

"No, I can tell you with one hundred percent honesty that Papa wrote it."

"But?"

"But... I may have been sitting beside him to dictate."

Sabra gasped and took the piece of paper, playfully hitting Cici with it. "You're incorrigible!"

"Hey, it's not *my* fault that when I asked to use some of my savings to pay for your wedding that he just went to your parents and offered to pay for the full thing. Kinda stole my thunder, you know?"

But Sabra just caught Cici's face in her hands and kissed one cheek than the other. "You're too good for this world, you know that?"

Cici felt herself blush, as she always did whenever anyone she admired complimented her. "Hardly. I was just lucky enough to be born to a family that has money. I figure it's kinda my responsibility to spread that luck around."

"There are plenty of people in your position who don't feel that way at all."

"And that's why you're not friends with those people."

Cici didn't go into the fact that she knew plenty of people like that too. Especially her Texan cousins. Thankfully, that whole part of the family seemed to turn that whole schtick around, but that didn't mean that she was ready to be buddy-buddy with their patriarch. But the sons were all alright, and their brides. Cici didn't know them overly well, but whenever she'd met any of her in-laws, they'd always been fun to sit and chat with.

Also... absurdly attractive. Cici didn't know if her cousins were picky or just had insane luck, but she didn't think she'd ever seen a prettier collection of people than when she went to family reunions. It always made her feel so little and underdeveloped. At least with everyone popping off babies she was no longer the youngest Miller in existence.

But sometimes, she felt like she was still treated that way.

"Exactly. You can't be greedy and obsessed with money and be a good person. And I'm only friends with good people." Sabra tossed her hair over her shoulder and batted her eyes at Cici, which lasted an impressive collection of seconds before they both burst into laughter.

"Oh, I missed these times," she continued, leaning over and giving Cici a peck on the cheeks. "I know we always had our virtual dates, but it's not the same as being in the same room as you and goofing off."

Cici nodded, her heart full of the familiar love she had for her best friend since childhood. "It was like when they put us in all separate classes that one semester in sixth grade, but for four years."

Sabra shuttered. "Ew. Why would you even mention that awful time?"

"You're right. It'll stay buried right next to that time you puked all over Ms. Mathison's desk."

"Hey, you promised you'd never bring that up again!"

Now it was Cici's turn to bat her lashes. "Did I? Must have slipped my mind."

"Why you-"

Suddenly Sabra was out of her seat and Cici was too, the former giving chase around their small kitchen and dining room. It was silly, naturally, but that didn't matter because it was fun.

There was a reason, after all, that they'd always gotten along. Cici was aware that she was a little... different from other folks. Not in a particularly spectacular way, but just enough to be either annoying or overwhelming. She loved fantasy books and the adventures they would take her on. She saw magic in the cycles of nature and majesty in the fictional races of elves, dwarves and fairies.

And Sabra was much the same.

They never let the confines of being proper, fitting in or claiming 'normalcy' bother them. They just were what they were, and at the moment, they were having fun.

Or, at least they were until the door suddenly opened in front of Cici and she had to skid to a stop to not accidentally crash into one of Sabra's parents.

Now *that* would have been awful. Mr. and Mrs. Gamal had always been wonderful and kind to her, almost like a second set of parents. The last thing she'd want to do was bowl one of the aging adults over and break their hip or something.

Except it wasn't either of Sabra's parents at all.

"Oh, hey there you two. You running from a snake or something?"

"Baz, you know I haven't run from a snake since I was an eight-year-old girl," Sabra countered.

Normally Cici would have joined in on the banter, but normally she wasn't nearly face to face with none other than Baz Gamal, the man she'd had a crush on since she was old enough to know the meaning of the phrase."

"H-h-hey there, Baz..." she murmured, feeling her cheeks heat. Thankfully her awkward response was talked over by the two siblings and she had a chance to slink a few feet away.

After all, it wasn't her fault that Baz was wearing nothing but a tank top and jeans with splashes of oil and dirt across them. Or that his skin was glistening from the combination of sun and sweat and a good day's work. Or that his hair was as thick as ever and his eyes just as kind with a smile that could—

Okay... She was getting carried away.

Taking a deep breath, Cici took herself out of the doorway and headed to the kitchen. What better place to be if she was thirsty after all? Because, even if she still harbored feelings for her best friend's brother, that was squarely in the box labeled 'never gonna happen'.

Firstly, because he was the brother of her best friend. Cici wasn't the best at social mores, but even she knew that dating a sibling of a BFF was almost always crossing a boundary that wasn't supposed to be crossed. Secondly, because Baz had always made it clear how much he saw her as a little sister. Which, while being a major bummer, just showed how good of a person he was. Thirdly, perhaps the most important reason of them all, Baz was happily in love.

And not with Cici.

No, he'd been dating a cool musician and model who he met in the city that he eventually moved to. At first Cici had selfishly hoped they wouldn't make it, but after two years of happiness, she realized she was being bitter and not a good friend, so she let him go.

Or at least tried.

Sometimes she fumbled, like when she was suddenly confronted with the man looking like the star in an action movie, and those feelings would come welling up again.

"Cici, where did you go?"

Quickly, Cici grabbed three cans of soda and popped back into the entryway. "Just thought we could all use a drink!" she said. Of course her friend of two decades knew better, her eyebrow raising just enough to let Cici know exactly what she thought of *that* excuse, but thankfully she didn't leave Cici out to dry.

"Aw, thanks Cici. It's good to see you again; it's been a while," Baz said as he shot a sideways glance in her direction. Why did his have to sparkle like that?

"It sure has," she answered, trying not to stutter hard or blush. Funny, how she'd spent so much time becoming an educated, competent woman, but it only took a few minutes with a childhood crush to have her tumble to pieces. "Here ya go."

He took the soda, flicking it open and taking a long drink, before tipping his head again. "I actually came in here for a drink break, so this was perfect. I'll catch you two later."

"Later," Cici muttered, trying to sound normal.

Not that she really had an inclination of what *normal* was.

"Don't forget to come back in for sunscreen in a couple

hours," Sabra reminded him. "You've been in that cushy city garage so long that you've gotten all pale."

Cici had to double take at that. Baz was all copper skin that went gold when the sunlight hit it directly. He was *gorgeous*, in a sun-kissed and thriving sort of way.

"Only compared to you, ya hooligan," Baz shot back. "Some of us don't get to go swim all afternoon any time we want."

"Get an online job, and you can do the same," Sabra said with a sniff.

"Eh, I don't think I have the skill for interpreting that you do."

"There are other jobs."

"Yeah, yeah, I'm gonna get back to work before you badger me into a career change. See ya later, Cici."

"Bye…"

He left and Cici waited a long, *long* moment before returning to their previous seats and basically collapsing across the table's surface.

"Goodness, after all this time and all those cute college boys, are you still hung up on my brother?"

"Please don't tease me," Cici groaned into the table's surface. "I'm trying. He's in a relationship and I respect that boundary because I respect him. Sometimes, it's just harder than others."

"A relationsh—*Oh!*"

"Oh?" Cici asked, picking her head up. "That's a very particular '*oh*'."

"I'm sorry, Cici, but with the engagement and the wedding and everything, I totally forgot to tell you that they broke up!"

Cici sat there a moment, letting those words wash over her.

"They. What?"

Sabra leaned in, her voice dropping despite the fact that they were alone. "It's actually really awful. Baz found out she was cheating on him with one of his partners in the shop. Ricky, I think? It was a huge betrayal from both of them. That's one of the reasons he's back here for a couple of months rather than just a week or two before the wedding."

"*What!?*"

How horrible! Cici couldn't even imagine the shock and anger. She'd never been cheated on in her life because she'd never really dated, her heart hung up on a peg that she had a hard time getting off of, but it had happened to Charity and that whole ordeal had been truly terrible to watch her sister go through.

Cici's fist clenched at her sides as she thought about that woman not only cheating on Baz, but a friend that he trusted also doing that to him. What a complicated, messy situation. No one deserved that but least of all Baz.

"Can I break her kneecaps? Please tell me I can break her kneecaps."

"As much as I love you and also know that you could totally afford a lawyer if you did that, since when have you ever been the type to break anybody's limbs?"

"I could learn! Charity is a good teacher."

"I mean, if anyone could turn you into a baddie, it's her. Remember when she busted up a bunch of folks at the fall festival?"

"I have heard that story so many times, but it never gets old."

"Some things are classic."

Cici recognized that her friend was trying to lighten the mood, but her brain was stuck on the anger and shock of it all. Baz was the *nicest* guy, and not one of those fake ones either. And one of the reasons she'd backed off was because he was so clearly in love with his girlfriend. Like, nearly worshiped the ground she walked on, bought her flowers, gassed her up, and bragged about how amazing she was in a way that was both adorable and painful. Cici had always told herself that she was happy because Baz was happy, and that was what mattered.

"Anyways, back to having a dry wedding. How badly do you think people would revolt?"

"I think it's your wedding. Do what you want."

Cici tried her best to concentrate, but her mind kept returning to the injustice of it all. And then, underneath it all, was the little voice reminding her that suddenly, for the first time in literal years, Baz was *single.*

And wasn't that something?

$$4$$

Baz

When Baz first got home, he was worried he'd have too much to do between catching up with people and changing his schedule up. But after the first couple of days, whenever he slowed down enough to think, his thoughts would just go back to his ex.

And that was one subject he would very much like to avoid.

So, he'd taken to checking up and fixing his parent's car, then his own car, and the neighbors' cars. Once that was done, he started doing all the menial but tedious home upkeep tasks that his parents were having difficulty with as they were getting older.

Then, just as he was about to run out of those to keep himself occupied, Sabra came down with the flu. Baz didn't wish illness on his little sister ever, but if she had to get sick, well, she certainly picked a good time for it.

"Baz..." he heard his name floating down weakly from the stairs. While so far her symptoms weren't too serious, the last time he'd seen his sister she was sweaty, exhausted and tucking herself in for her third nap of the day. Clearly she needed some rest.

"Coming!" he called from the kitchen where he'd been in the middle of brewing some coffee. A couple of bounding steps later, and he was up on the second floor of their small house. "You okay?" he asked, ducking his head into his sister's room.

Oof. He didn't even need her to answer when he saw her. Her hair was a rat's nest around her head, her eyes were puffy, and she was covered in a layer of sick-sweat. Poor girl.

"Peachy," she replied dryly, ever his sarcastic little sibling.

"Yeah, I supposed I deserved that. What'd'ya need?"

She reached to her nightstand and patted a thick looking binder there. "Would you grab my calendar out of here and cancel all my appointments for the week? I'm definitely gonna need a couple of days to sweat this out and recover."

"Should I try and reschedule them for you?"

"Don't worry about that. Just apologize to them for the inconvenience and tell them that I will call them as soon as I'm feeling better to reschedule."

"Wow, and they'll just go with that? Letting you cancel last minute without having to pay?"

"Apparently. Amazing what the Miller name can get'cha, isn't it?"

Oh *right*. Baz had forgotten that the wedding was being sponsored by the Miller patriarch. He was a great guy, for all that he always seemed so lonely. But losing the love of his life could do that to a person.

"It really is. I'll take this downstairs and make sure it's handled. Why don't you take a nap?"

"Oooh, now you're speaking my language. I always knew there was a reason I kept you around."

Baz let out a short laugh. "Yeah, you needed someone tall enough to reach where mom hides the good snacks and someone to open all those pickle jars."

But Sabra's face softened, and her clammy hand reached out to gently pat his shoulder. "No, you're so much more. I hope you know that. You're an incredible big brother and always have been."

The compliment came out of nowhere and Baz felt an instant surge of both embarrassment and pride. He was glad he was well tanned from the summer months, otherwise he was sure his cheeks would be a blazing red.

"Clearly all those meds are getting to you. Get some rest."

"No, seriously, Baz. You're amazing. I've heard horror stories about big brothers and what they put their younger siblings through but you're nothing like that. I always knew I could come to you if I was in trouble or needed help. Especially when I wasn't sure if our parents would understand it."

Baz didn't know what to say. He'd entered his sister's room for a simple favor and ended up getting (somewhat delirious) accolades. When even was the last time he'd gotten a real compliment? The experience was so foreign he almost wanted to use the impressively thick binder as a shield and high tail it to the downstairs.

"Uh... you're welcome?"

"Alright, I can see I've made it awkward. Just give me a five-feet away air hug and then you can go recover downstairs."

"Even on your deathbed, you are still a gracious patient."

"That's it! You've lost your air hug. Get thee gone, heathen."

Another laugh bubbled its way up from Baz's chest and he couldn't remember the last time he'd laughed so much consecutively. It was... nice.

"I'll be up later with that tea. Sleep well."

"Love you, you big meanie."

"Love you, you little twerp."

Baz shut the door and headed back to the kitchen table. By the time he sat down, his hand was achy from holding the brunt of the massive binder's weight.

"Let's get this crackin'..."

Despite Sabra's cheery assurances, Baz had definitely thought there would be more trouble with the cancellations. But it turned out that mentioning Papa Miller's name really did carry a lot of weight. It was so easy to forget that the family was insanely wealthy with a dynasty that stretched across half of the continent. They really kept themselves humble.

Well, except for those Texas cousins, but Baz had been lucky enough to only have to deal with that particular Miller uncle a single time.

So, Baz went down the list, proud of himself for how quickly it was going, until he hit a very specific appointment the next Wednesday.

Lunch date with Cici.

A slow, nostalgic grin spread across his features. Cecilia Miller was Sabra's best friend for life. Her BFF, as they constantly said when they were preteens. Or 'ride or die', which he was pretty sure was the current popular phrase. The two had met in elementary school and had been inseparable ever since.

Baz knew, as an older brother, it was expected that he would harbor some sort of 'too-cool-for-you' exasperation for anything involving his sister or her young friend, but Cici had been a good kid. A little weird, but a good kid.

She'd always been attentive and excited about whatever Baz did, whether that was getting into cars, soccer or action flicks. Baz recalled several nights of babysitting her and his sister while they all watched spy movies that were probably a bit too mature for them, laughing and eating popcorn.

Geez, when was the last time he'd talked to her? When had so much life slipped away from him without him noticing? He'd let so much fall to the wayside and for what? A girlfriend who cheated on him and managed to bring it into his work as well?

Disappointing... To say the least.

Pushing down the bitter ire that rose in the back of his throat, Baz took a breath and dialed Cici's number.

She answered almost immediately, her voice sounding surprisingly chipper. Not that Cici wasn't a happy person, but usually she wasn't quite so bright, especially before lunch.

"Whoa, Baz, what's up? Long time no text."

"Oh hey, you know, trying to escape the grind. But hey, I was calling because Sabra's gonna have to cancel on you for your lil' lunch date."

"Huh? Is everything okay?"

"Mostly, but she's real sick right now."

"Sick!? Like her allergies getting bad again?"

"No, we're pretty sure it's the flu. You know how she is once she gets sick."

"Are you sure it's the flu? Has she been to the doctor? What if it's pneumonia? Or an infection of some sort?"

Normally Baz would roll his eyes at someone being so over the top with something as simple as the flu, but with Cici, he got it. She'd been real young when she'd had to watch her mother die, and that was something that was bound to give some people some hang ups. If she wanted to go all mama-bear on Sabra, well, Baz would let her.

Especially considering what the family had had to go through more recently with Cass. Sabra had kept Baz up to date on everything about that awful situation.

"It's just the flu. She's doing alright, she just needs to stay hydrated and get some rest."

"Hold on a sec for me, would you?"

Before he could even respond, he heard her calling out to someone else in the room. "Hey Clara, can you make some of that sick-people tea and soup?"

"Hey, Cici, that's alright. You don't have to do that."

There was a faint answer from who had to be Clara, and then Cici's attention was back on the phone, like Baz hadn't objected at all.

"Okay, I'll be over in the next day or so to drop off a care package. Give Sabra all my love, will you?"

Baz's heart gave a little squeeze, both happy that his little sister had such a great friend but also feeling a bit guilty about the help, even if he wasn't asking for it.

"Hey, I don't want you to have to make an extra trip. I'll just come pick it up."

There was a moment's pause. Barely there, but just enough for Baz to pick up on it. Had he said something wrong? Eventually, however, Cici answered with only a slight bit of trepidation to her tone.

"Uh... sure. Yeah! That would be convenient. Besides, you haven't been to the ranch in forever!"

That was certainly true.

"What time works best for y'all. I know the rest of your family is early birds, but—"

"Actually, I've been improving on my sleep schedule a lot. I'm usually out and about to help with chores and have coffee in the garden around eight am."

Baz's eyes widened at that particular revelation. "Eight am? If only your freshman year public speaking professor could see you now."

"Actually, I'd be happy to never see him again in my entire life, thank you very much." She let out a sort of wistful sigh before recovering. "How about eleven? Does that work for you?"

"Sure, I can do that."

"Alright, I'll see you then. Talk to you later."

Baz responded in kind and then she hung up, leaving him to the rest of the cancellations. He doubted any of them would come with healing soup and tea, but hopefully they could be just as easy.

5

Cecilia

Baz was coming over.

Baz was coming over!

BaZ wAs CoMinG oVEr!

Cici stared at her ceiling, trying not to reverberate herself out of existence.

The man she'd had a crush on from the ripe ol' age of eight was coming to her home the very next day to pick up a care package. She was going to have to see him without his sister around. To interact with him. To act like a completely normal, well-adjusted adult.

Oh no.

"Relax, Cici. It's gonna be fine. You've managed to be normal around Baz for most of your life."

Well... normal was relative.

But it wasn't like she had always been a hopeless mess around him. Not at all. But she hadn't seen him since she'd forced herself to get over him and respect that he was in love with someone else.

And sure, yeah, they were broken up, a news-bomb that Sabra had so graciously dropped right onto Cici's brain. But that didn't mean the shape of her, the echo, wasn't still there. Baz's ex was a gorgeous, well-spoken woman with a smile like a movie star. A plus size model with a massive following on social media and multiple magazine campaigns. She'd even been on the cover of several magazines and billboards in Times Square.

Nothing like Cici.

No, Cici would never be anything like that. She wasn't graceful. She wasn't glamorous. She was just... well, *Cici*.

For a long time, she'd harbored resentment towards the beautiful woman who'd so thoroughly rooted herself in Baz's heart, but after their second year together Cici had realized she either needed to be a good friend or be a stranger.

Naturally, she'd chosen to be a friend.

But that was so much easier to do with only the occasional digital exchange with the handsome man. It was also much easier to do when he was actually dating and happy. But seeing him face to face and newly single was... well, it was a lot.

"It's fine, it's fine," Cici chanted to herself, like if she said it enough that she could brainwash herself into thinking so. "Just take a nap, have a nice night in the family, and when you wake up tomorrow, you'll realize that none of this is a big deal."

Except when Cici woke up the next day, it still was very much a big deal.

"Crap."

Sliding out of bed, Cici found herself much more on edge

than she'd been the day before. "Relax. It's just your best friend's older brother who's coming over. That's it. No need to freak out."

Except she was freaking out a little, internally.

Cecilia had done a lot of work on her anxiety since the years when her panic attacks had been overwhelming, but she could feel the familiar battery acid taste of one on the back of her tongue.

"Alright, Cici, five things you can hear, four things you can touch, three things you can see, two things you can taste…"

Slowly, she worked her way through it until she could think clearly again. However, it wasn't so much thinking clearly as much as it was just thinking more about Baz.

"…I'm a mess."

He was newly broken up with and recovering for goodness sake! She was supposed to have gotten over him! And yet her heart was doing that very specific ache that was reserved solely for pining over the mechanic.

"Yup, a *real* mess."

But just because she was an emotional mess didn't mean she had to be a physical one. Slipping out of bed, she splashed some water on her face and threw overalls on before heading off to the chicken coup.

"Oh, hey there! You're up early."

Cici blinked at Clara, who was fully dressed and already had a basket held in the crook of her elbow with her hair in victory rolls. How did she do that? It was barely past eight am.

"Uh, yeah, I was actually hoping that you could help me do my hair and makeup?"

"Ooooh, is there a special occasion?"

"…no."

"And this wouldn't have anything to do with a certain mechanic being in town?"

"...You're far too busy to be so up to date on gossip, Clara."

Her older sister grinned brilliantly, striding forward and looping her free arm through Cici's. "Please, it got the little old ladies of church to stop talking about Nathan and me for about twenty minutes, how could I not know?"

"They really gossip about the two of you?"

"I certainly spend a lot of time at an unmarried man's house for an unmarried woman. I even spend the night." Clara said the last time in a dramatic whisper, as if she was uttering unspeakable horror, before cracking up into laughter.

Cici couldn't help but roll her eyes. Even if Clara was sleeping with Nathan, it wasn't anyone's business but their own. Granted, the middle Miller sister was as committed to waiting until marriage more than anyone else Cici knew, so it wasn't like anything was going on.

Unless...

No. Cici shook her head. She didn't want to dedicate any of her brain space to wondering if her sister had changed her decision or not. Besides, Cici wasn't entirely sure how she felt about the whole thing anyways. She planned on waiting until marriage. But when she caught glimpses of her sisters and the love exchanged between them and their men... well, she can't help but feel a little envious.

But that was probably more of an after effect of meeting the love of her life when she was eight. Except she wasn't the love of *his* life.

Tragic.

"Hey, you okay? You drifted off there."

"Yeah, I'm fine. Just got a lot on my mind."

"I understand. Nothing some strategic eye poking with a black stick can't solve."

"Wait, you won't really poke me in the eye, will you?"

"Not unless you wiggle as bad as you did last time."

"...I'm in trouble."

"THERE YOU GO. PERFECT."

"Hardly, but there's beauty in imperfection."

"Is that one of those artful phrases they teach you in college?"

"Learned that one on my own, believe it or not."

They shared a chuckle and Cici felt that warm familiarity of being home. She'd missed bantering with her siblings, missed being a part of their closeness. While she didn't regret and was incredibly proud of her accomplishment with her degree, it was nice to finally be in the new chapters of her life.

"Well, Baz will certainly be impressed when he sees you, that's for sure." Cici gave a noncommittal hum, but it was too late, Clara was already spinning off into one of her romantic, old-timey fantasies. "Goodness, I remember how you used to moon over him, all big eyed and blushing whenever he paid you any attention. It really was adorable."

"Yeah... adorable..."

Cici could remember all those times too. It was burned into her brain. And so was the moment when she was thirteen and watching reruns of *Family Matters* only to realize she was quickly heading into Steve Urkle territory, and she never wanted to make Baz uncomfortable.

"I remember the three of y'all would go swimming together,

and he'd cook you food whenever you spent the night over at Sabra's house. It really was... oh. Why do you look like you swallowed a lemon?"

I guess it's too late to school my expression now.

"Just thinking about all the eye poking you threatened me with. Turns out you were all talk."

But Clara didn't take the bait, instead crouching to look into her sister's eyes. "What's wrong, lil C? You—oh. *Oh.* You're still in love with him, aren't you?"

Cici did her best to breathe deeply through her nose. She heard that helped dry up tears if one's eyes were watering. It helped. Sort of.

"Love is a strong word," was all she managed to get out flatly, staring in the mirror in front of her.

She looked pretty. She did. Not that she didn't look pretty without makeup, but she liked the polished sort of veneer that Clara always managed to give her. Emphasizing all the parts of Cici's face that she already liked so much. But at the current moment, she couldn't help but feel a bit silly for getting all gussied up for a guy she was supposed to be over.

"I'm sorry, Cici, I didn't know. I thought it was, well... something you'd grown out of."

She reached in for a hug but Cici dodged it by standing up with a shrug. "It's fine. Baz isn't attracted to me in that way, and he's both found and lost the love of his life. It hurts from time to time, but I truly want him to be happy, even if it's not with me. That's what matters."

"I... I just... I'm sorry. That's all I can say."

"It's okay, but that's the reality I've gotta live with. I like his company even if it can never be romantic."

"That's a real good way to look at it."

"Yeah, I like to think if there's one thing Papa taught us, it's that a true friendship is never a waste, even if it doesn't go exactly how you wanted it to."

"Ain't that the truth. Although I feel like I could make a whole book out of all the good sayings and principles Papa has taught it."

"Write it then! Become famous, change the world and make millions."

"Haha, I don't think it works that way."

Cici shrugged again, but more for humor than her previous despondency. "How do you know if you haven't tried?"

"Alright, well after I get all the repairs done on Nathan's homestead, I'll hop right on that."

"Don't think you're slick. I live on a ranch. There is no 'done' with repairs. Not ever."

Clara narrowed her eyes in a mock scowl. "And here I thought you might have forgotten about farm life now that you're a fancy college lady."

"I'll never forget how you like to use that pretty face to be sneaky, dear sister."

"Sneaky! How dare you. I am, uh... conversationally creative."

"Haha, more like conversationally persistent."

"I'm totally stealing that."

"It's all yours."

Cici didn't even realize that they'd been walking as they bantered until they were out the door, arm in arm once again. Blinking, she felt a sense of calm wash over her as they traversed across the ranch. She was home, and even if tomorrow wasn't guaranteed, she knew her family always was.

That was one of the joys of being a Miller. Having money

was nice, and Cici would never deny her privilege of never having to worry about it, but that was nothing compared to the love and warmth that was woven into every part of her life. She didn't know what she'd do if she was one of the Texas Millers— although their family had made improvements by leaps and bounds.

...Uncle Clint was still a giant butt though.

"Nothing important. Where are we even going?"

"I figured you needed some distraction and I'm pretty sure there's some weeding to do in the garden, so I thought I could kidnap you for at least twenty minutes before you realized what was happening."

"You fiend! See what I mean! Sneaky, sneaky!"

Clara just twirled and did a bow, laughing as she did. Cici clapped, cheering for an encore until they both heard someone pulling up to the front of the house.

"That's Baz, I suppose. I could always run the soup and the tea out to him for you."

That was true Clara, always the gracious one willing to help. Cici had always admired her older siblings for how much they seemed to be paragons of goodness. It was hard to measure up to Charity, the head of the household who directed everything, could fix anything and had a mean right hook. Cass, her second in command and the organizer who had survived the impossible without ever giving up. Charlie, who was wherever anyone needed him, ridiculously good with horses, and had dealt with a severe trauma from college all on his lonesome. Then Clara, the perfect gardener, animal husbandry expert, and killer pin up with an amazing sense of style and sewing ability.

Where did that leave room for Cecilia Miller? When she was younger, Cici had been fine with being the baby, the one that everyone protected and watched over. She was the one who was fragile and cherished, especially after their mother passed away.

Maybe it was puberty that made her realize that she wanted more. Maybe it was seeing that Baz, as independent and strong as he was, didn't want a partner that needed to be babied. That being swaddled in bubble wrap and gentle treatment made him look that at her like more of a little girl than a potential partner.

Granted, considering that Cici was a couple of years younger than him, she had actually been a little girl for a bit.

"Hey there, Cici! Long time no..." Baz's greeting had started out normal, but as he rolled down his window, he trailed off. Instantly Cici wondered if she had something in her teeth or on her face. "Uh, see," Baz finished, clearing his throat.

Oh dear, it was going to be awkward, Cici could already tell.

"You been keeping yourself busy?" He managed to sound more like normal and Cici pushed her rising nervousness down. She was Sabra's best friend and Baz's kinda friend, she could be normal for ten whole minutes.

"Yep! I always love this time of year. Never any dull moments!"

"I would think you'd want a few of those after all the craziness your family has been through."

She let out a half-hearted chuckle. Yeah, he was right, but laughing seemed too eager, too desperate. "Well, we haven't had a car wreck, anyone try to blackmail us or sudden deaths in the family for over a year, so I'd call that a win."

"I'm glad you can say that with a grin; I was worried I went a touch too far there. Hanging around mechanics all day has made me a bit insensitive at times."

"Is it that or are you just getting old..."

Baz laughed outright at that and Cici felt like she was on

better footing. They'd always had a pretty teasing relationship, with Cici quipping against him, but Baz could always give it as good as he got it if he wanted to.

"Excuse me, I'm only twenty-seven. I'm not *old*."

"But you are nearing thirty. Before you know it, you'll be over-the-hill."

"And who says there's anything wrong with that?"

"Nobody, as long as you're okay with gray hair and wrinkles."

Baz couldn't answer right away, his eyes going wide as a loud bark of laughter erupted from his mouth. "Now that's just not fair!"

"In case you haven't noticed, life isn't," Cici said with a sniff, assuming a hoity-toity head tilt until she couldn't hold character and giggled too. Goodness, an actual giggle. She hadn't done that since she'd gotten all flustered over her professor asking to submit Cici's essay to a contest in sophomore year of college. "Get used to it."

"Yeah, yeah. You got this miracle soup or not, Miss Fountain of Youth?"

"It's in the kitchen. You can follow me."

"Sounds good to me. It's been a hot minute since I've been here."

"True."

Baz got out of his car and Cici was struck by how much he'd filled out. He'd always been a strong boy, with biceps she'd drooled over as an adolescent girl, but working at his shop in the city had definitely increased his frame. Gone was the wiriness that often went with young men, replaced with a sturdy sort of solidness that Cici couldn't help but notice.

And *boy,* did she notice.

"Wow, this brings back memories, doesn't it?"

"Yeah, it does."

Cici lead him around the kitchen island where he'd once studied for his permit test with Papa while his parents taught a traditional dance to the rest of the kids in the house. There, right on the counter, was one of those fancy thermal travel pots that Clara had invested in and a large thermos.

"Here you are! One magic soup pot with a side of magical healing tea."

"Perfection. Where's Clara? I should probably thank her in person."

Cici tried not to feel a pang of jealousy, because that would be absolutely ridiculous. "Last time I saw her she was in the garden out back."

"I remember hanging out there in the thick of summer." Baz looked around, and Cici could see the nostalgia shining bright in his eyes. "Man, I didn't realize just how much I missed this place. It's really been far too long. I guess it's easy to forget stuff that used to be important to me when I've got my nose pressed to the grindstone."

His words hung around Cici, echoing in her ears. He missed the ranch? He considered it important? The very thought made her flush and she was now trying to think of some sort of reasonable response. But then Baz was talking again.

"You know, would it be presumptuous to ask you for a tour of the place? Or at least a lil' meandering?"

"Of course!" Cici agreed far too quickly. But if Baz thought anything of it, he didn't say so. "Come on, I think Sabra will survive a few extra minutes waiting for her soup."

"She's passed out like a rock, to be honest. I say we've got a couple of hours before I should wake her up and get some tea down her throat."

"Sabra was always terrible about taking her medicine," Cici mused. She remembered the one time her entire family got the mumps only for Sabra to catch it right as Cici was almost recovered. At first Sabra had been a real mule about following any of the doctor's instructions, but after Cici cried about losing her mother and not wanting to lose her best friend too, Sabra had finally acquiesced.

"She's gotten better, but she still takes a little coaxing."

Cici nodded and they fell into other memories as they walked through the garden. It was like the images of their childhood and young life were etched into the leaves of the squash or inscribed into the cucumber vine. Instead of memory lane, it was more like a memory garden, full of laughs, aches, learning, and so much growth.

So much growth.

"You know, I can't believe you."

Cici blinked, wondering if she'd said something particularly boneheaded, only to see a grin on Baz's face. "Come again?"

"I know it's silly, but it's crazy to me that you're a real, grown adult right now."

"Well, I don't know about a fully grown adult. I still feel a little underbaked. You know, adult-light." Cici was excited to hit a quarter century, but three of her siblings were already over thirty, so it was hard not to still feel like a youngling compared to all of them.

"Hah! Adult-light! I love it! Sometimes I feel that way myself." His expressions sobered a bit. "I worry I've made the wrong choices and I'm behind everyone else my age. That I'm never gonna be able to catch up because I put all my eggs in the wrong basket."

"What? No! Don't think that way, Baz. You're amazing!" It

had been a long time since Baz had confided in her so frankly, and Cici couldn't help but feel both flattered that he trusted her as well as hurt for him. She understood what he was talking about, it was entirely similar to how Charity had sounded after her divorce, but she hated that he felt that way.

"Haha, you have to say that, you're my little sister's best friend."

Ouch. Cici wasn't exactly thrilled at that level of separation. "I'd like to think I'm your friend too."

"My friend? Of course!" And then there was that beaming grin again, bright and white against his tanned skin and dark, dark stubble. "I'm just saying, I get feeling like not-quite-an-adult."

Cici nodded, wanting to say more, but her tongue was so heavy in her mouth. Funny, she was always known for being effervescent and verbose through her whole college career, but being back home in front of her childhood crush had her words all twisted up in a mess above her head.

"Hey, isn't that Charity's workshop?"

Cici blinked and looked ahead to see it was indeed her sister's little shack away from home. "Sure is."

"Let's go see what she's working on."

"You mean you wanna see if you can hone in on one of her projects like you used to when you were a teenager?"

He winked and *goodness,* if that didn't make her almost pass out right then and there. Heart thundering, Cici tried to cover up her sharp intake of air with a cough.

So much for being an adult. She was acting like she was a wee little kid again with a crush bigger than her own brain.

"I mean exactly that. Come on!"

His speed picked up and Cici found herself jogging to keep

up with him. Good ol' Baz; he really loved whenever he could get his hands on something mechanical. Cici had never really had the mind for that stuff, but she'd always enjoyed watching him or Charity work like they were a pair of particularly gear-minded alchemists.

The loud, rock music reached their ears before they made it to the door and Cici winced. Charity was going to end up ruining her hearing before she was fifty with how loudly she liked to blast her stuff. For being such a mother bear to the entire family, she sure was bad at taking care of herself.

Maybe Alejandro would finally be able to talk some sense into her on that front. He was a doctor, after all.

"Hey, Charity! What's this? Working on a classic truck?"

Cici jumped back to reality, not even realizing that she'd drifted yet again. What was it about Baz that made her feel so unmoored? She didn't really have any idea. But Charity was already sliding out from under the truck in her shop, a wide grin on her face.

"Whoa, Baz! What are you doing here? It's been years, buddy!"

"You didn't hear? I'm back in town for a few months to prep for Sabra's wedding?"

"Man, I probably did but I forgot. Nothing happens in a small town without everyone knowing, so *someone* had to have said something."

"That is how the grapevine goes, or something like that." Baz was being friendly, but Cici could already tell his attention was almost entirely on the truck. "So, what's this you're working on?"

"You don't remember?" Charity asked, her grin fading ever so slightly.

Baz shook his head, but Cici knew. It was Papa's truck, the

same one he'd had when Mama was alive. It had been worked on and worked on and worked on, to the point that it was probably in better condition than when she'd passed. No one in the family talked about why it was still around, but Cici was pretty sure that it was kept because of all the memories of driving the love of his life everywhere and he wouldn't ever be ready to lay those to rest.

Poor Papa. Cici wanted him to move on and find happiness, she really did, but it wasn't like she could lecture him on the subject considering that she'd been hung up on the same guy for sixteen years. Who even did that?

No one sane, that's who.

"Uh... It looks familiar, but I work on a lot of cars," Baz answered a bit sheepishly.

"I suppose that's true. But this is Papa's truck. Just doing some maintenance, an oil change and toppin' up some other stuff."

"That's why it rings a bell!" Baz said with a clap of his hands. There was a lull for a moment before he looked pleadingly to Charity. "Say... you wouldn't mind some help with this, would you?"

Cici held her breath, almost worried her sister would say no, but Charity's broad grin returned in full force. "Sure, why not. You know where the tools are, so gear up."

"Really? You haven't changed them in eight years?"

"Why would I? Cass worked out the perfect organizational system here and I think she just might kill me if I messed with it."

"Fair enough." And then Baz turned to Cici, his megawatt smile on full display. Cici felt her knees do that crumbling thing again and she leaned against the truck to support herself. "Hey,

Cici, you wanna grab us some drinks from the mini-cooler and pull up a seat? We always used to hang around together for projects. It'll be just like old times!"

He remembered that? "Of course!"

Cici rushed over to the coolers to grab a beer, a sparkling water and a glass-bottled cream soda, proud that she could remember both of their drinks of choice. But by the time she made it back over to them, they were already deep in conversation about their plan of action.

But Cici didn't mind. She sat the drinks down where they would see them when they broke their concentration then found herself a stool to perch on while she listened, watched and occasionally handed things to them.

Or threw things at them, if they were soft enough.

It really was like old times, and before any of them knew it, the minutes were slipping away into the hazy embrace of nostalgia and productivity, a heady mix if there ever was one. It wasn't until Charity's phone began to shrilly ring that any of them even thought to check a clock.

"Holy halibut! How did an hour and a half pass?" Charity blurted, draining the rest of her beer. "Doing all this work made the time fly, I guess."

"I hear that's what happens when you're having fun," Baz joked right back, wiping his hands on one of the towels that Cici had tossed him just a bit earlier. "I suppose we should head back."

"Probably. Before your sister sends out a search party."

"I don't think she's even got enough energy to do that."

"In that case, you probably *should* go," Charity stated, wiping her own face.

"We left the soup in the kitchen," Cici added. "You better not forget it, or you'll be turning around and doing this whole trip again."

"Can't have that, now can we?" But then there was that strange... well, *strangeness* to his tone again and suddenly Cici felt like he was seeing her *too* much. Too keenly. Too presently.

...maybe college had messed her up.

No, that was probably the pervasive night terrors and panic attacks growing up.

"Definitely not."

If Charity noticed the suddenly awkward sort of pressure of the situation, she didn't say anything, just began cleaning up. Cici appreciated the reprieve and began heading back to the main house with Baz.

He was quiet too, with neither of them saying anything until they entered the kitchen, where Clara and Dani were already talking and laughing with a small lunch spread laid out in front of them.

"Hey there, Cici, I was worried you guys forgot the soup!" Clara said, putting her fork down and standing up to her full height. It was a subtle move, but it brought Dani fully into view, and Cici didn't miss how Baz' eyes lingered on both of the women ever so slightly.

It was nothing disrespectful, not at all, but there was a light of interest there, of appreciation, and Cici felt a small wave of rejection bubble through her.

Right. Baz likes bigger women.

Cici wanted everyone to love their bodies, and she recognized that both Clara and Dani had been bullied about their size, but for a moment she wished that she was fuller figured like them. After all, Baz's ex was a plus sized model that he'd met when she was shooting in a junk yard while he was there collecting scrap and looking for parts.

Ugh. Cici had worked really hard and gotten a lot of therapy to be happy with herself and it was a bit worrying that so much of her confidence and center was already crumbling. She needed to get a hold of herself before she returned to her uncertain and unstable teenage self.

Being an adult was so complicated!

"Hi, I'm Dani! I'm married to Benji, one of the sons from the other Miller clan."

She offered out her hand and Baz took it, beaming. "I remember hearing about you guys! You all here for a visit?"

"We're actually helping Charity and Alejandro build their own house here. Benji has been looking for more practice before we make an addition onto our own house."

There was a jerk from Clara and suddenly the middle sister was staring at Dani with that piercing gaze that happened whenever she was sleuthing something out.

"What? Do I have something in my teeth?"

"Why do you two need more room?"

"I mean... I don't feel that's a particularly shocking thing-"

"You're *pregnant,* aren't you!?" Clara drew in a sharp breath and clapped her hands while Cici could only stare openly at the two.

Dani's eyes went wide, and she rushed to hush Clara. "Shhh! We're still keeping it on the downlow!"

"Sorry, sorry, I just..." Clara's eyes went to Dani's belly and Cici couldn't help but feel sorry for her middle sister. Her romance with that Nathan fellow was going fantastically, but they weren't anywhere near marriage or starting a family. Cici was well aware that Clara had an ardent love of babies. "It's so exciting. I'm so happy for you!"

"We're very excited, but we're just taking it slow, you know, just in case."

Clara nodded and Cici's attention returned to Baz again. She expected a sort of polite boredom, something that usually came whenever an unmarried bachelor was subjected to baby-talk. But instead, Baz looked like he was keenly interested, almost wistful.

Wait, did Baz want a family? Or was he just feeling melancholy over the future he'd lost with his ex?

It was certainly something to think about.

And she instantly thought about it, her mind launching itself into what it would be like for Baz to have several minis running around his home, in charge of his very own shop. It was easy to see and it made her heart yearn in a way that was well over painful, and yet she didn't want to stop. A terrible habit, really, and Cici tried to shove that mental image away. But still, as Baz sank into warm conversation with the two women, Cici couldn't help but wonder why she liked to torture herself so.

6

Baz

"Soup's here," Baz announced as he strode through his family's front door. Before the last syllable was out of his mouth, his mother was taking the container and setting it on the stove.

"Ey, Mom, I can do that myself. You can take a rest."

"I've been resting all weekend. Now I want to take care of my baby."

Baz didn't even try to fight his grin. He knew not everyone was lucky to have parents who loved them so wholeheartedly, but he'd always be grateful about how they were still Mom's babies, even if they were full grown.

"Mom, I love you to pieces, but with your diabetes and you being a little older, you probably should keep your distance from Sabra a bit. The flu is no joke."

"My baby is sick and you want me to stay away?"

"Physically, yeah. I'm here and facetime exists, Mom. I promise you, Sabra will be happy that you've taken care of yourself. The last thing she'd want is the knowledge that she made you sick."

Baz waited while his mother considered his words, and eventually she moved away from the oven with a sigh. "Alright, fine, but you tell her to call me as soon as she's awake and has the energy. I miss the sound of her voice."

"Of course, Mom. I'm sure she misses you too."

With a quick kiss to the cheek, his mother nodded and wandered up to her own room, no doubt to take a well-earned nap. Baz busied himself with making some toast and heating up the soup and tea only to find that they were still plenty warm from the fancy containers Clara had sent them in.

"What kind of technology is this?" Baz mused to himself, shaking his head. The Millers certainly never did anything by halves.

But thinking about Clara made him think of the ranch in general, and he felt himself plunge down into his thoughts with all brakes cut.

Since when had tiny, nerdy, Cici Miller grown up so much? She'd always been a slight, daydreaming little thing, full of dreams bigger than her own body. Her head had been permanently in the clouds when it wasn't plunged into the horror of a panic attack or night terror, and he'd remembered plenty of adventures from having to pull her and his sister back to earth.

But he'd met a *woman* on the ranch. One confident in herself with an easy grin and a mischievous glint to her trademark Miller-intense eyes.

Scientifically, Baz was well aware that people grew up, but he hadn't seen Cici since her freshman year of college. Suddenly being confronted with a graduated (with a Masters!) adult had put him off center. Cici had gone and conquered the world while Baz had ended up cheated on by the love of his life and betrayed by his own business partner.

So much for being a good example to her.

Or maybe he was a little too much in his head. It was easy to take a negative slant on everything considering all that happened with his ex and his business partner, but he didn't want to wallow. Life was just too short.

The toaster practically ejected its bread and Baz grabbed it, wincing as the heat made its way through his thick callouses. Quickly, he buttered it before assembling the rest of the meal and taking it up to his sister.

He had to admit, it smelled *really* good. If his sister weren't really sick, he might have been tempted to steal a bowl for himself. But as it were, he was pretty sure that Sabra needed every ounce of Clara's magic soup and tea that she could get.

"Look who's back. I thought I was going to have to send out a search party."

Baz grinned at his sister's weary quip and the fact that her best friend had said the exact same thing. She had a bit of color to her cheeks but otherwise looked just as clammy and tired as he'd left her.

"What can I say, those Millers are a charming bunch. Time just moves differently around them."

Sabra let out a weary but agreeable sound. "That much I know. I go over there for lunch, and the next thing I know Papa is teaching me how to properly prune a tomato while Clara is preparing a four-course dinner."

"You sound like you're talking from experience."

"Oh, you know I am."

Baz set everything on her nightstand before leaning over to prop up her pillows so she could sit up a bit. What he meant to do was ask her how she was while he was tending to her, but instead, an entirely different question came out of his mouth.

"So, I saw Cici."

He should have known better than to try to play nonchalant. Sabra caught his tone immediately and her eyebrow raised, albeit wearily.

"And?"

"Why does there have to be an 'and'?"

"Because with you, there's always an 'and'. You never talk just to talk."

Baz rolled his eyes, but he didn't try to deny it. "She looks, uh, healthy."

"Right. Healthy. I'm absolutely sure that's exactly what you mean."

"Why are you such a twerp?"

"Excuse you, I am twenty-five, I am far too old to be a twerp. The term you're looking for is busy-body."

"Right, I'll keep that in mind." Baz also meant for that to be that, but then his mouth was off and doing its own thing again. It certainly liked to do that. "But man, she's grown a lot."

"Well, it's been years since you saw her not on a phone screen. Mostly we've been having virtual hang outs."

"Yeah, I guess I knew that, but still, it was pretty shocking. Where's the little miscreant I used to have to fish out of trees or pull back from traffic?"

"She's been grown a while, Baz."

The reminder was gentle, but it reminded him of just how much he had missed. He had only moved to the city three years ago, how did it seem like a lifetime had passed? Sounded like some wibbly-wobbly, messiness.

"And so have you, I suppose."

"I mean, I am getting married. Assuming I survive this plague."

"Dramatic," Baz teased with a huff, handing her some tea.

"And I've won awards for being that way, don't you forget it."

"Like you would ever let me."

They shared a chuckle and a gentle sort of quiet fell over them while Baz watched her sip her tea and nibble on her toast.

"Don't forget the soup. Clara made it, of course."

"Don't you worry, I'm just working my way up to it. Who knew merely existing could be so exhausting? I'm gonna need a nap just from working up the gumption to sit up."

"Good. You need to sleep more anyways."

"Please, if I wanted to be lectured, I'd throw myself into the hall so Mom can smother me with good intentions."

"Speaking of which, she wants you to call her later."

"Huh?"

"I told her she shouldn't come in here because she's still getting her diabetes under control and I don't want her getting sick, so she compromised only if you let her do her smothering virtually."

Sabra snorted into her tea. "Thank goodness for modern technology."

"It does allow certain conveniences."

Sabra nodded but the conversation dwindled, his sister obviously worn out by all the energy she'd already exerted. Baz tried not to do his own smothering, but he did wait until she signaled for the soup, then carefully handed it to her. She managed to get down about half, groaning about how good it was as she did, before she finally let out a weary sigh.

"I think that's all I can do right now. Gonna sleep again."

"You do that. Text me when you're up, I'll bring up water and more soup."

"You're a champion, brother. I'm so glad to have you back."

"Great, your fever is making you all nice again. I'm getting out of here before you get all mushy on me."

"Heaven forbid I compliment my own brother."

Despite the germs, Baz leaned down and placed a kiss on his sister's sweaty, heated forehead. Whatever, he had a pretty strong immune system as it were.

"I'll see you later."

"See you."

At that, Sabra cuddled further under her mountain of covers while Baz headed downstairs. But as much as he tried to stay in the moment, his mind kept going back to Cici and how perfectly grown she had looked.

Times were changing, that was for certain, but Baz felt so left behind.

7

____

Cecilia

It took Sabra two full weeks to recover to one hundred percent and somehow Cici managed not to over-whelm her with attention the entire time. It was a personal best for the youngest Miller, but she was only so strong, so when her best friend called and said they were due to have an entire day together to reschedule everything that was cancelled, Cici jumped on it.

And if 'jumping on it' involved baking a blackberry crumble with Clara and cooking some thick cut steak with roasted pota-toes and fresh veggies from the garden... well, that was just how things happened.

"There's my best friend!" Sabra said the moment Papa opened the doorway, practically throwing herself into Cici's arms. Cici hugged her in kind, but she couldn't help but notice that Sabra was a bit thinner than when she'd last left the bride to be. Sabra had never really been very good about being sick, but she'd always been excellent about bouncing back afterwards, so Cici was confident she could get back to her wedding dress size in no time.

"And there's my best friend! How are you? Can I get you some water?"

"Actually, I wouldn't say no to some of that ginger-mint tea your Papa made for us a while back. You still have some?"

"Oh yeah, I'm certain we do. Here, come to the kitchen, I'll brew some. You want it hot or iced?"

"Iced please! I've had enough hot liquids to do me for a year or two, although I'm super grateful for them, I'm ready for my chilled drinks again."

"Hah, I totally understand."

"Also! I was wondering if, on one of our breaks, we could go visit the chickens? I miss their clucky little faces."

"I'm sure I can make that happen."

"Awesome!"

It was good to see Sabra back in such bright spirits, but Cici could still see a certain sort of weariness to her friend when she finally sat down on one of the stools at the kitchen island.

"How's the fiancé, by the way?" Cici asked, realizing she tended to forget to include him in conversations that weren't specifically wedding related. He was a lovely man, really, but Cici and him weren't close, not like she was with Sabra.

"He's doing great, practically glued to me since I've been feeling better. I thought he was gonna combust when I told him he couldn't visit me during the worst of it."

"Well, he is a doctor. I'm pretty sure he's used to putting his health on the backburner."

"For his patients, yeah, but I've always been pretty strict about that boundary. I'm his partner, his safe haven. I don't wanna be another extension of his work."

Cici nodded, smiling softly. Some thought Sabra over dramatic or emotional, but Cici loved how thoughtful she was, how she stopped to think about how everyone might feel and put great weight in that knowledge. It'd always made Cici feel so... *valid.*

"I get that."

"But yeah, anyways, aside from death-by-smooches, it's been alright. He actually dropped me off here on his way to work."

"He's still on that four days on, three days off schedule, right?"

"Yup, still renting a hotel and then coming home Friday-Sunday. It's not ideal, but taking that job three hours south of here meant an over 20K increase in pay. It's not something either of us were able to say no to."

"You think you'll move there eventually?"

Cici meant to ask that question lightheartedly, but there was no answer. At least not verbally. Instead, she felt arms wrap around her torso and her friend's head resting on her shoulder.

"Don't worry, I'm not gonna take off and leave you. You're stuck with me for at least another five years."

Cici wanted to say that wasn't long enough, that she wanted her best friend with her forever, but she also knew that was far too selfish a thing to ask.

"I can do with five years."

"There ya go. Remember, always the bright side."

"Because life is dark enough without seeking out the shadows."

"Exactly."

Cici exhaled a long breath and let her shoulders relax. Sabra wasn't going away, and they were both lucky enough to live in an era where technology could let them talk to each other even when they were far apart.

"We should start planning. There's never enough time in a day."

"Ain't that the truth!"

After a bit more prep, the two of them sat down and started up the call list. People were relatively pleasant, and Cici expected a bit more pushback or difficulty rescheduling, but nine out of ten of them were a breeze.

"Huh, you know I heard that people in the wedding industry are awful, but everyone's been so pleasant here! Well, except the seamstress. But she's a seamstress, stress is literally in the name of her job."

But Sabra let out a short laugh, shaking her head like Cici had said something funny.

"What? What's so amusing?"

At that Sabra blinked several times. "Wait, you were serious?"

"Yeah, why wouldn't I be?"

"Cici, people are being nice because you're a *Miller*. I thought you were just being facetious and pretending like you didn't know why."

"Because I'm a Miller? None of these people are from this town, how could they know about our family?"

Sure, Cici knew that most of the town knew about the Millers and their little clan, but it wasn't like they were Kardashians or paparazzi mongers. The last huge news had been during Cass's accident.

"Hun, I know you folks like to keep it low key, but your

cousins literally own a massive dynasty business in Texas and are basically socialites. Not to mention one of your cousins is married to Chastity, who's a huge internet personality."

"...right."

Cici was well aware of the weight her name brought, but she guessed after being away at an Eastern college for so long, she forgot just how far their reach went. "Huh. I didn't think about that."

"That's alright. I'm certainly not complaining."

"That's good, because I can't change that, I guess."

For a fleeting moment, that ever-reaching shadow of the Miller name and reputation loomed over Cici once more, but she shoved that down and forced herself to move past it. She was more than just her family name. She's proven that with her degree and basically living out on her own during her entire college career.

...but sometimes that still didn't feel like enough.

"By the way, your sister sent me an email asking for another fitting. Do you think I should do one now, or wait until I get back to my normal size in a week or two?"

"I definitely think you should wait," Cici answered, glad from the distraction from her melancholy thoughts. "Although I'm sure Clara would actually like the busy work if she had to take it in then let it out again."

"She sure does love to sew. I thought she was gonna be upset when my fiancé hired a seamstress for all the men's stuff for the wedding."

"Nah, she doesn't like men's clothes as much as women's anyways. She says too many straight lines and not enough variety."

"I feel that. Men usually don't have to know the difference

between a shirt, a blouse or a chemise and which one is event-appropriate."

"I... I'm not sure on what the difference is between those."

"Well, that's not surprising."

"Hey!"

Sabra jokingly blew a raspberry like they were little kids again, so Cici dipped her fingers in her glass of water and flicked it at her friend. That moment of levity was enough to thoroughly derail the pair from their goal, and before Cici knew it, they were scrolling through pictures of fantasy wedding dresses online.

"Hey, knock-knock! You're not answering your phone!"

A familiar voice drifted in from the front of the house and Cici sat bolt upright, her eyes going wide. "Is that Baz?" she asked, suddenly keenly aware that she was dressed only in an oversized t shirt and dirty sweatpants.

"Huh? Oh! My phone!"

Sabra scrambled to open her handbag, letting out a swear or two as she checked it. "Ag, he called me like three times! I didn't realize so much time had passed." Quickly, she stood and rushed towards the front of the house. "Coming!"

Equally as frantic, Cici rushed over to their needlessly shiny and chrome refrigerator, checking out her reflection. Patting down her stray hairs, she managed to get herself slightly on the right side of slovenly before Sabra returned with her brother.

"Hey, Cici. How ya doin'?"

She hadn't seen him since the last time he'd picked up soup for his sister, but her heartbeat spiked for a moment like it had been months. She really was hopeless, try as she might not to be.

"Oh, you know, just living." What did she even mean by that? Cici certainly didn't even know. But Baz gave her a knowing nod. "You hungry?"

"Always."

"Lucky for you, I've got the solution for that."

"You always do." He gave her a crooked sort of smile while her brain went haywire for a moment. She always had a solution for being hungry or she always had a solution in general? Was that good or bad? And why was she suddenly caught up in analyzing everything he said?

"How's a sandwich sound?"

"You gonna put potato chips on it?"

He remembered that? "I haven't done that since I was a preteen."

"Seems like a terrible habit to break."

Cici chuckled, feeling her cheeks color ever so slightly. She certainly felt a bit like a preteen with how many butterflies were fluttering around her stomach. "Okay, one cold cut sammie with some potato chips coming up."

"Oooh, it's not often I get a Cici made meal," Sabra said, plopping right back in her seat. "Usually, Clara has full dominion over the kitchen."

"Clara's over at her beau's place, so you've got me, I'm afraid," Cici said, going about getting all the fixings out.

"That's not a downgrade," Baz said nonchalantly, sitting down next to his sister. It was a compliment, there's no doubt about that, but it was said so matter of factly that it snuck right through Cici's defenses and went straight to her heart.

"You don't have to butter me up, I'm already making you food."

He might have said something back, but Cici quickly opened the fridge and stuck her head in like she was looking for something. Maybe that way she could cool off, both literally and figuratively.

Alright, Cici, get a hold of yourself.

Sabra was her best friend. Baz was her friend. Maybe it was just the giddiness of being back home and in the swing of things that was getting to her. So often the ranch seemed like a mystical world set apart from everything else, a place where the outside reality had no dominion, and everything was that much headier.

Yeah, that was it. The foreignness of being a graduate was fading and she was just slipping back into her old habits like putting on a pair of well-worn and comfortable slippers. That was all.

Or at least... she hoped that was all.

Mostly recovered, Cici extracted herself from the fridge and went about actually making the snacks she was supposed to. Maybe it was having something to focus on, maybe it was her pep talk, but Cici was able to respond to conversation like an actual human being. It was a welcome change, and she felt herself settling slowly the more they chit-chatted.

"Hey, Cici, do you know what that magical soup Clara made was? Smelled like chicken noodle, but it was so much more than that! Like richer, and heartier."

Cici grinned at her best friend. "That was mean-rooster stew. It's a rarity considering that Papa and Clara are very careful about which roosters they let guard the flock, but every now and then a newcomer decides to ruffle a few too many feathers."

"Mean-rooster stew? You mean..."

"Yup, it's made out of an aggressive rooster. We don't mind them protecting the ladies, but if they try to attack us with beak or claws more than once, then they gotta go. Papa believes far too many young children are traumatized by mean roosters and they're utterly unnecessary if you have the proper protections in place."

"I didn't even know mean roosters were a thing!"

"I've seen videos on it," Baz said with a nod. "I just always thought they were sensationalized since all of your chickens here are so nice. Well, except for Mrs. Nesbittle. She was always a cranky one."

"I can't believe you remember Mrs. Nesbittle!" That particular chicken had been a wonderful lady with crossbeak, meaning she needed a special watering and feeding container. She was messy, short tempered, and only liked Papa, Clara and Cici.

No one understood why the crossbeaked birdie included Cici in her small circle of acceptable humans, but she'd actually been a lovely bit of company. She would run to the front door to meet Cici after school and would usually putter around if Cecilia did her homework outside. Clara had a theory that Mrs. Nesbittle knew where she was needed, but that was a very stereotypical Clara romanticism.

"How could I not? We spent a lot of time here, the three of us. I always thought I was lucky that if my lil' sis had to make friends with another annoying little kid, it was you."

Well, that was certainly a mixed bag. Cici wasn't thrilled on being called an annoying little kid, but the back of her mind reminded her that she was *very much* an annoying little kid, complete with debilitating panic attacks and bursting into tears at a moment's notice.

"Please, you know you loved hanging out with us."

"I loved being paid by mom to watch you, yeah."

"...you still think mom paid you?"

Cici felt her eyebrows shoot up to her hairline. Sometimes being next to Baz and Sabra was a bit like being stuck in a convertible on the highway, and she had a feeling she was about to get a real show.

"What do you mean do I still think mom paid me? She gave me money every week." Sabra began to chuckle, and Baz looked incredulously from her to Cici.

"Do you know what she's talking about?"

"...maaaaaayyyybe," Cici admitted ever so slowly.

"What's going on here? Don't tell me there was some vast babysitting conspiracy I didn't know about."

Sabra chuckled again; eyes full of that mischievous energy that always meant Cici was in for a fun time. "No, nothing like that. But Papa Miller paid our family a stipend every month. He said it was for feeding Cici, paying for movies and gas and all that, but a chunk of it was always supposed to go towards you every month."

"Wait, he really... How did *you* know about this and not me?"

"I dunno, it came up a couple years ago. Mom let it slip when she wasn't thinking clearly one day."

"I've known about it since I was a teenager," Cici said. "Papa was worried I'd take it the wrong way, but I thought it was great."

Baz let out a long breath, shaking his head. "Man, I'm feeling like I went through half my life with blinders."

"You were a teenaged boy, of course you did."

That startled a sharp laugh out of both Cici and Baz, which cut the last of the tension. Between sandwiches, tea and plenty of stories, her heart was full and her cheeks hurt from smiling so much.

And with every moment that passed, it was harder and harder to shut down those feelings that were rapidly bubbling upwards.

8

———————

Baz

Baz whistled to himself, in a thoroughly good mood as he organized his parent's mess of a tiny garage. He missed his shop and all the space he had back in the city, but he wasn't ready to go back to that place at all.

In fact, he didn't know if he'd ever—

RING!

"Why is the shop calling me?"

Staring at his phone like it might explode at any moment, Baz debated answering it. Part of him wanted to throw his phone in the closest body of water, but another was curious.

What could they possibly want?

Against his better judgement, Baz flicked his thumb to answer the call and brought it up to his ear.

"Hello?"

"Hey, Baz, I hate to do this, but we have an insane emergency here and we need you."

Baz didn't answer for several moments, his head reeling. He hadn't expected to have to deal with anything regarding his work and the people there, so having that suddenly thrust on him had his brain slowing down to about two working cells.

"Baz?"

Right, he should probably speak. "What's going on?"

"We have this hot shot guy in who's willing to pay triple to get his ride taken care of today, and it's one of those obscure ones that you love. Seriously, none of us understand the system at all."

A dark, very angry voice inside of Baz wanted to let out curses until his phone spontaneously combusted. But instead, he took a deep breath and thought about it.

His ex, Victoria, had cheated with his business partner, Red. Baz and Red had been friends all through high school and vocational school, and the both of them had gone in on the garage in the city.

The owner had been selling it at a huge discount because so much was in disrepair or outdated, but the two of them still couldn't afford it. Instead, they'd been able to work out a deal where he and Red bought half of it, and the owner kept the other half, and together the three of them had been able to revitalize the business and bring an entirely new consumer base in.

It had been a dream come true. An amazing livelihood that kept growing and growing, with plenty of potential for the future.

But Red had gone and ruined it.

The key word was *Red* ruining it, however. The three other mechanics and the original owner hadn't done anything wrong.

It wasn't like *they* cheated with Victoria or kept it a secret. In fact, it was Terry who'd given Baz the heads up when he thought something suspicious was going on.

"...I could probably come help out."

"Really!? Oh man, you have no idea how much I would appreciate that. This guy is a real diva and I was half tempted to kick him out, but Terry says that he has a lot of connections in the hotrod and car shows."

"Yeah, I gotcha, it'll take me about an hour and a half or so to get there."

"No problem! I'll tell him! You're a lifesaver, Baz. And for what it's worth, we miss ya here."

"I... thanks. Oh, and Skillet?"

"Yeah?"

"Make sure Red isn't there."

"Don't worry. He knows he's not welcome on the premises."

What? Baz hadn't known that. That was certainly an... interesting development. For some reason he'd expected the shop to play more neutrally between the two of them. "That's good to know."

"Of course, see ya later, Baz-brain."

"See ya."

Hanging up, Baz took a deep breath. If he had his way, he'd never have to go anywhere near anything that ever reminded him of Victoria ever again.

Too bad life didn't work out that way.

Despite all his dread, when Baz rolled up into the shop, he felt a small trickle of familiarity run through him. Ever since

Victoria had shaken his world up, he'd been a bit adrift, his entire future and all his plans suddenly turned inside out.

Multiple friendly greetings sounded as he made his way to the front desk where, sure enough, there was the guy. Baz didn't even need to be introduced to him; he could spot him from a mile away. Dressed in needless designer clothes with an air of bravado that only came from having more dollars than braincells.

...maybe Baz would luck out and he'd be of the decent sort. Like the Millers.

Except Baz knew that he was never lucky.

"Finally. Do you have any idea how long I've been waiting?"

"You're gonna have to wait a lot longer if you continue with that tone, sir," Baz said matter of factly. He swore the whole shop practically ground to a halt at that with the other couple of mechanics there staring openly.

He couldn't blame them. Baz was known for being the diplomat of the group. Whenever there was a difficult or annoying customer that pushed other people past their limits, it was Baz who was called on.

Well, that wasn't going to be the case any longer. Baz had gone through far too much to be disrespected by someone who was asking for his help.

"Pardon me?"

"I'm here to help you sir, but I can just as easily ask you to leave where you can find someone else certified in your vehicle. But, considering that it's already past noon, you'll be hard pressed to find someone who can do this today."

With every word out of his mouth, Baz felt a bit emboldened. Like a dam was released inside of him and he was finally saying so many things that he'd always wanted to say.

"And as a matter of fact, you should know that we might not even have the parts you need. I tend to horde specialty things because I'm that kind of guy, but if I've got to order what you need, well... it is what it is."

Baz watched as the man turned several interesting shades. He expected him to either turn around and leave or throw a total fit, but instead he seemed to actually physically swallow his ire down and speak in a relatively level voice.

"I'd like you to take a look at it, if you could."

"No problem. Now, I was told over the phone what was going on, but why don't you walk me through it from your perspective?"

It took some effort, but Baz was pretty sure that he actually managed not to sound smug as he said that. There would have been a time, not too long ago, where he just would have stood there and let the man be rude. He'd always thought he was taking the higher ground before, but really, it just always seemed that the conflict that would come from standing up for himself wasn't worth the effort.

Baz wasn't sure what changed, but he was pretty sure that he liked it. The world had changed plenty since he'd become a workaholic, maybe it was time for him to change too.

9

Baz

Days passed after the shop called him in without any more contact and Baz didn't know what to feel about that. He also didn't know what to feel about the fact that his baby sister's wedding was marching ever closer.

He knew she was a grown woman. In fact, he saw her as a grown woman and was proud of her. He *respected* her. And yet when he saw her trying on reception dresses, or picking out drapery colors for the wedding table, he couldn't help but see the precocious little sibling he'd spent so much of his life taking care of.

Not that his parents had been absent, no, not at all. But they'd come over from the United Arab Emirates right before they had Baz. They were just as much a part of that world as they were the US and had the complex experience of being first generation immigrants.

But Baz and Sabra? They were born in America and citizens, and they'd been in the unique position of being between their parent's realities and their own. Two peas in a pod.

Plus Cici.

And perhaps, a bit more often than he'd like to admit, Baz's thoughts went to Cecilia Miller. Little Cici wasn't so little anymore. He felt more aware of her than he'd ever been before, but he didn't know what to do with that information.

For example, suddenly he was keenly aware of how she was the only Miller sister who was small and petite. And it fit her perfectly.

Gone were her oversized clothes that she'd inherited from her siblings, and instead she wore simple fitted t-shirts and jeans. Well, except for when he caught her in dirt covered overalls.

Except even her chore overalls were different than what Baz remembered. Cici was by far the least curvy of her sisters, but her form was undeniably feminine.

And he kept noticing it.

It wasn't even that they were spending that much time together. In fact, the little flashes they had together never seemed to be enough. Like there was more to say, or do, or *feel* and never enough time.

Strange, to miss someone he hadn't really thought of much in the past few years. Why had he let his friendship with lil' Cici Miller fade so much?

Oh right. Victoria.

Well, Victoria and work. Baz was well aware that he was a bit of a sap. He loved spoiling his love and showing her she was special. He'd really thought that Victoria was the love of his life, so he'd dedicated himself to providing her a future that he thought was worthy of her.

And she'd slept with his best friend and business partner.

As if life had it out for him, his phone rang again, and he saw it was the shop. It figured, they were the only ones who called him besides his parents. If Sabra wanted to talk, she'd text him.

"Hey, what's going on?" he said as he answered. If it was another 'emergency' he was going to tell them that they needed to start turning people away. Sure, it was nice to tell that man off from before, but it wasn't something Baz wanted to make a habit of.

...even if it was very satisfying.

"Man, Baz, that rich dude is back and he's mad as a hornet."

Baz recognized Skillet's voice and he let out a long sigh. "What's he want? Got another classic car that needs maintenance immediately?"

"Nah, man, he's claiming you bricked his car!"

At that Baz had to clamp down on his anger, which rose red-hot and whip-sharp in his chest. He didn't have much of a temper, but liars and cheats certainly got to him fast.

"Alright, I'll be there in an hour and a half. I'll try to talk him down. But it sounds like this guy doesn't know how to take care of his cars and wants an out."

"Yeah, I'll make sure to call Mr. Baxtin and have him come out too. We need all the backup we can get."

Baz winced at that. He didn't like having to call in the original owner if he didn't have to. But if moneybags was as angry as Skillet was making him sound, then it definitely wouldn't hurt to have him present. "Yeah, sounds like a plan. See you soon."

There had once been a time when the shop was his home,

right? Where he felt comfortable, safe and happy within his walls?

Who could say? He had a feeling that time was much farther in the past than he'd realized, but he just hadn't wanted to admit it to himself.

ONCE MORE BAZ found himself striding into work in what was supposed to be his sabbatical. Normally he could never afford to take several months of work off but returning the engagement ring that he had bought over a year earlier as well as adding in the money for the surprise trip to Hawaii that he'd been saving up for had given him a lot of wiggle room. That, *plus* the money he was saving from staying with his parents and subletting the apartment he had previously shared with Victoria, *and* all the vacation time he'd accrued had given him a solid cushion so he could get some distance and figure some stuff out.

Except it was hard to have actual distance when they kept calling him back.

Frustrating.

So yeah, maybe that irritation built up in him a little more quickly than usual, because when he saw the guy standing in almost the exact same spot in the front of the shop, Baz could feel his forehead already beginning to heat.

He was going to be a real pain. Baz could sense it.

"You ruined my car! I'm gonna sue the pants off this place."

"I assure you, I didn't," Baz responded calmly. "Although I'd be more than happy to double check and help you figure out what's going on."

"I'm not letting you touch my car again! You ruined it!"

"Sir, when you left you said the car was running better than it ever had before. Accidents do happen, but I need to look at your vehicle before we can confirm anything."

The man continued to grumble but Baz ignored it, going outside to give directions to the tow truck driver. The fact that moneybags hadn't been able to drive the car back to the shop was certainly alarming, but Baz was almost certain he hadn't done anything that could cause total catastrophic car failure in less than two weeks.

No, something else was definitely up.

Baz was so in his head, backtracking over everything he'd done that day, that he didn't realize Skillet had approached him until he practically ran into the taller mechanic.

"Whoa, sorry about that. I was just thinkin'."

"Nah, man, it's okay. I just wanted to say, I think it's great how you're standing up to that dude. He's a real pain."

"Yeah, he's not exactly a gracious guest."

"But seriously, man, you used to always just endure those folks. I've never seen you just lay it out like that. I got mad respect for you."

Baz had just been thinking as much before, but it was certainly something else to hear Skillet say it outright.

"Thanks. I, uh, I guess I just got tired of people taking certain liberties."

"I gotchu. You always have been like, legit, one of the chilliest and understanding dudes, but sometimes you just gotta... ya know, lay down the law. It's nice to see you doin' that."

"I guess I just hit my limit."

"I got that, I got that. You been through way too much, man. With, ya know..."

"Oh yeah, I know." Victoria. It didn't even need to be said.

And although it was a sort of a glum topic, Baz felt a flicker of pride. Of accomplishment. "And thanks, brother. I know I haven't been around much but, well, you get it."

"Yeah, I do. Take as much time as you need, bro."

"Thanks, man, I appreciate that."

Baz was well aware of the reputation that mechanics had, but Red, the original owner and him had all been very picky about the workers they brought on. Some were a little rough around the edges, but they were all good folks. Skillet especially, who basically was a big Cajun softy who'd moved to the area five years previously so he could be closer to his kids. Baz could respect that. Sometimes romantic relationships went south but children? Those bonds were supposed to be forever.

With a little bit of lightness in his step, Baz headed over to where the tow truck was pulling up, watching as Jose and Terrence were getting it into position. Moneybags was pacing in the opening that led out to the parking lot and Baz did his best to ignore him.

Eventually the car was in place and Baz was able to get under the hood. It didn't take him long to figure out what was going on, and once he did notice the problem, he gritted his teeth.

He was in for a fight, alright.

Trying not to alert the customer, he waved Skillet over.

"Hey, you need me?"

"Nah, but were you able to call Mr. Baxtin?"

"Yeah, he's on his way, why?"

"This guy was totally slipping the clutch and the flywheel's got all sorts of cracks. His transmission is also basically trashed. If I had to guess, he's been bad rev matching nonstop. I don't think this guy actually knows how to drive stick."

"Ain't that the way with these rich yahoos? They spend all their money on these nice cars then ain't got no idea how to drive 'em." Skillet made a sucking sound through his teeth, shaking his head. "If I had a car like this, I'd treat it like a real lady."

"Calm down, Skillet. Wouldn't want your girlfriend getting jealous."

"You kidding? She's just as much as a gearhead as me. But she's more into monster trucks than hotrods."

Baz nodded, letting out a long breath. He could joke around with Skillet for hours, the guy was chill, but he had a soon-to-be-nightmare customer to deal with.

"Tell me when Mr. Baxtin gets in. I'd put money on this guy threatening to sue and he's the only one who has the clout to get him to back down."

"Ugh, I wish you could just tell him where to shove it, but I get it. Rich people rule the world and all that."

"Hey, I'm just happy to own a third of this place. I don't care that moneybags like this guy don't realize or respect that."

"Right on, man, right on."

Skillet headed off to do a standard oil change but thankfully, Mr. Baxtin didn't take too much longer to show up. He was dressed in his usual suit and was carrying an actual briefcase, which almost made Baz laugh.

Mr. Baxtin was a character of a character. A rich, self-made man, he wasn't a mechanic at all and had actually originally started up the business for his son, who was a mechanic. But in one of life's many tragedies, his son died suddenly of a pulmonary embolism out of nowhere, and the man was left with a company he didn't have the expertise or interest in.

It had been plenty clear that he hadn't been quite ready to

sell the place when Baz and Red came on, which was probably the only reason he'd agreed to the three-way split. But with all of them as equal owners, Baxtin could come in and sit in his son's old office every once in a while and handle the paychecks, while Baz and Red handled the rest.

Since he was old money, he had all sorts of connections that no one else in the shop did, and he was used to slinging around with people who liked to threaten to sue or lawyer up at the drop of a hat. Which was exactly the sort of expertise that Baz was going to need.

Exchanging a knowing glance with Mr. Baxtin as he came in, Baz headed over to Moneybags, who was still pacing.

"Well, can you fix what you did?"

"I didn't do anything, sir," Baz said as calmly as he could.

"What do you mean?"

"You've been shifting improperly and damaging parts of your clutch from using it incorrectly. Your transmission is also suffering. You'll need a replacement flywheel at minimum, and that's definitely a part I'll have to custom order."

"That's ridiculous! You bricked my car!"

"No, sir, I did not. In the two weeks since you left, you have caused intense damage to your car. Normally these kinds of issues take months to build up, so may I ask, did you go on a cross country trip? Perhaps speeding along the interstate for several days in a row?"

As the man's face grew more and more red, Baz didn't need him to answer to know he was right. The man had totally gone on a weeklong joyride and messed up his car in the process.

"You're just trying to dodge this! I'm gonna sue your pants off!"

"Sir, if you want to get me out of my pants, you should buy

me dinner first. It'd be a lot faster than going through the courts."

"What!?"

The man was shocked, which was the entire point. Sometimes with entitled rich folks the best tactic was to surprise them and disrupt their rhythm. It was one of the best ways to deescalate.

"Is there a problem here?"

And that would be Mr. Baxtin. Baz didn't even have to turn around to imagine how the older, built man in the suit with his salt and pepper beard looked standing just behind him.

"Your employee is incompetent and destroyed my car! Do you have any idea how much these cost?"

"My employee? Sir, you are speaking to one of the owners of this shop, not an employee." Mr. Baxtin's hand landed on Baz's shoulder, and he couldn't help but wonder what kind of father the older man had been back when he'd had the chance. "Baz, what's the story behind this?"

"I did some basic repair and upkeep but this gentleman decided to go on a long trip without learning how to properly shift."

"Huh, that's a real shame."

"That's not what happened! This idiot—"

Finally Mr. Baxtin took a step forward past Baz, towering over moneybags. "As a co-owner, I do not allow abuse in my shop. You may leave, now, or I'll be calling the police immediately. And if you'd like to take this to litigation, I have a lawyer on retainer who takes special interest in dealing with scammers."

"S-s-scammers?"

"Yes. So, I suggest you order a lift from one of those fancy ride-share apps and get out of our shop before I hit you with a trespassing charge. Do you understand?"

The man sputtered a few more things, most of them words that shouldn't be repeated in polite company, but he did decide to go ahead and leave.

"Don't forget to arrange a tow of your vehicle with your chosen company!" Mr. Baxtin called after him.

"Thanks, Baxtin. That went a lot faster with you here."

"No problem."

"You know, I just want to say I really appreciate you just taking my word for it."

The older man gave a sage nod. "I trust you, Baz. You should do the same for yourself."

Huh.

10

———

Cecilia

"Do you think I should let this dress out a little? I'm gonna be two months farther along."

"Didn't your sister hardly gain any weight with her pregnancy?"

Cici only half listened as the other girls of Sabra's bridal party talked amongst themselves. It wasn't that she was being anti-social but considering that she was the only Miller daughter in the whole group, she figured it would do her well to listen and get to know the other ladies she was sharing Sabra's special day with.

There was Lisa and Gemini, both from Sabra's college, and Lisa was newly pregnant. Clara had made her dress larger with plenty of shirring in it to accommodate for her growing womb, and Cici was quite impressed with how fashionable it looked.

Clara, of course, was living the absolute dream. She had four women all at once to dress up and fuss over. And the *wedding dress*. Clara had truly outdone herself on that work of art.

While Sabra's nuptials weren't an outright themed wedding, there was a heavy fantasy influence. Sabra's dress was the most beautiful, deep blue and a somehow coherent mix of her middle eastern heritage, American style and some classic elvish design thrown it. It shouldn't have worked, but it did, and Cici had a hard time not drooling over it whenever Sabra was in it.

Her fiancé was going to lose his mind when he saw her walking down the aisle. Cici was sure he was going to cry and she knew she'd probably lose it when that happened. There was something special about a new groom moved to tears by his bride.

Would anyone ever look at Cici that way?

Probably not. But that was okay. She could be happy for her friend anyways.

"So, what's it like living on a farm?"

Cici looked up from where she was absently sketching out Sabra as she stood in front of Clara's mirror, getting her fitting done. While she wasn't really that gifted of an artist, she loved doodling little memories in her journal. It was like snapshots of happiness that she never wanted to let go of.

"It's busy," Cici said out of habit. She'd been asked that question about a million times from a million people, and few of them ever *actually* wanted to know what ranch or farm life was like. "A lot of dirty work."

"Sabra said you had goats? Do they, like, faint?"

Why does everyone think that all goats faint?

"No, they're not that breed. We've got Lamanchas, mostly, some Nubians. We just recently got a pair of giant Boer goats that we plan to have a meat herd from instead of just having our milk herd."

"I have no idea what those are," Lisa said, laughing slightly, but Gemini leaned in with bright interest in her gaze.

"Wow, so you're able to raise an animal and then eat it? I always worried I'd never be able to do that part."

Another question Cici was used to. "It's part of the circle of life. We're very respectful and use the entire animal, from head to toe. I think too many people are too far removed from where their food comes from and that's disrespectful of the sacrifice animals give us."

"Wow, I never thought of it that way. That's a good way to look at it!"

Cici felt the slightest of color to her cheeks. She was always fiercely proud of her family's ranch, but she wasn't used to someone young and as clearly stylish as Gemini showing such outward enthusiasm.

She just hoped it wasn't one of those moments that people were actually making fun of her and she couldn't tell. Cici hated when that happened, although that hadn't happened in at least several years.

"Thanks. I like it. I couldn't imagine any other way of living."

"That's awesome. I feel like so many people aren't content with their life. You have something special."

Cici's cheeks colored further and she ducked her head a little. "Aww, thank you. You're being sweet."

"Nah, just saying it how I see it. I've just always been that way." Gemini laughed, tilting her head back so that her long, electric blue tresses caught the light just right. "And speaking of being honest, I heard that Sabra's brother is singlesville! I think I might wanna take a stab at that hottie with a body, if you know what I mean."

And there went that warm and fuzzy feeling.

"You're not his type," Lisa said bluntly, rubbing her barely there belly with a sort of absentmindedness that Cici thought was kind of cute.

"What do you mean? I'm a makeup artist, I can make myself into anyone's type."

"He likes big girls, I thought everyone knew that."

"Big girls?"

"Yeah, you know. Curvy. Brick houses. Stacked to the nines."

With every adjective out of the woman's mouth, Cici felt her mood sink a bit further. She was basically describing Clara, Dani or maybe even Charity to some people, but not Cici. Papa said that Cici took after her mother, who had been a taller, more svelte figure, and normally she took great comfort in that.

Normally.

"Huh, well a preference is a preference, after all. I know plenty of guys who have a main type but will deviate every so often."

...wait, really? That was a thing?

"Oh yeah? You looking to do a little deviating with Sabra's brother?"

"Lisa! When you say it that way it sounds gross!"

"Dating your friend's brother is kind of gross."

"Pppft, whatever. I'll still flirt with him when he comes around and we'll see if he's receptive or not."

Crossing her fingers, Cici sincerely hoped that she wouldn't be around to witness that interaction. For someone who was supposed to be over Baz but was very blatantly not, she didn't know if her heart could take it.

"Wow, what an amazing but tiring day," Sabra said as Cici pulled up to her house. She'd borrowed Charlie and Clara's jeep so everyone in the bridal party could fit in, and she was seriously considering buying herself a minivan. Especially since Charity was using her truck more and more to do stuff with Alejandro and Savannah while Clara was visiting Nathan almost every day.

"Yeah, it was certainly something."

Thankfully the conversation had quickly moved on from Baz and his preferences and willingness to stray from them, so Cici hadn't had to sit there awkwardly and pretend she wasn't somewhere between bothered and heartbroken.

"What are your plans for the rest of the night?"

Cici put the jeep into park and thought a moment. "I'm supposed to go home and do my normal chores, but Charlie and Daisy are both home and they usually finish things on their own if I text them. Why?"

"After everything you've done for me, you've got to be crazy if you think I wouldn't invite you in for dinner."

"Aww, you softy."

"What can I say? Besides, it's been ages since my parents got to eat a sit-down meal with you and they've been complaining that their third child has abandoned them."

Cici had to laugh at that. While she loved Papa though and through with every fiber of her being, she'd always felt that Mr. and Mrs. Gamal were kinda like a second set of parents.

"Alright, you've convinced me."

"Yay! The first full family meal in years!"

It wasn't a new idea, and yet Cici's heart squeezed in the best possible way, just like it did every time that Sabra confirmed their close friendship. Maybe it was leftovers from when anxiety ruled her life, but Cici would never take for granted how easily Sabra would declare how important they were for each other. It reassured her even when that dark, very mean voice inside her head liked to get particularly insidious.

Hand in hand, they went inside, and although Cici had just seen Mrs. Gamal a week earlier during the afternoon, the matriarch threw her arms open wide.

"Little Cici! You are here at sundown. Does this mean you're staying for dinner?"

"If you'll have me."

"Have you? Yes, yes, come it has been so long since we last had a true meal together. I made *fatayer,* it has always been one of your favorites."

"Everything you cook is my favorite, Mama Gamal."

"Oooh, you sweet thing. We need you around more often! You whip my babies into shape, make them much nicer to me."

"That's cause we're jealous that you spoil her," Baz said, descending the stairs with that megawatt smile that was completely, entirely unfair to everything in Cici's being. How was she supposed to concentrate when he was flashing that beaming grin all willy-nilly? "Not that she doesn't deserve it."

Some lizard part of Cici's brain must have somehow been immune to his flattery, because the next thing she knew, she heard herself responding. "Of course, I deserve it. I'm fantastic."

"Clearly," he said, brushing past her to give his sister a quick kiss on the cheek. "My parents have excellent taste, after all."

"Excuse you, what about me?" Sabra objected, pinching him.

"Ow! I come to you with love and this is how you betray me?"

"Oh, I'll show you betrayal!" Sabra grabbed a butter knife and brandished it like a sword. Perhaps it would have been alarming from anybody else, but for her, it was par for the course. "Have at thee!"

"But I am unarmed! You wouldn't cut down an unarmed man, would you?`"

"I'd do it in a heartbeat!"

"Cheeky."

Cici couldn't stand on the sidelines anymore. Grabbing a fork, she playfully jumped in front of Baz. "Fear not, fair maiden, I have come to save you!"

Anybody else probably would have told the pair that they were being ridiculous, but instead Baz let out a hearty, wonderfully warm laugh. "My hero!"

"You think that you can stop me?" Sabra said between her own peals of mirth.

"I know it!"

They began to very slowly mock-sword battle with their utensils. It was silly. It was stupid. But it was exactly what she loved so much about her friends.

"Ay, ay, ay, what have I told you about adventures at the table?"

It was Mr. Gamal's voice that cut in, amused but reproachful.

"Sorry Dad, I guess we got carried away. It's been a real fun day."

"I can't wait to hear all about it. Now, come give your father a hug, yes?"

"Only if you promise not to cry when I tell you about my day."

"You are my baby girl, and you are getting married. You do not get to deny me all the crying I want."

"Fair enough."

Cici's heart warmed yet again as her best friend embraced

her father, but she was surprised when Baz sidled up to her conspiratorially.

"You know, it really is amazing we turned out as good as we did considering how much our parents let us get away with."

"Maybe your parents know they can let you get away with a lot because you're so good."

"Aw, shucks. Here I was trying to be cheeky, and you've got to go and compliment me."

"Well, you've got an awful lot to compliment."

Wait.

Did she just say that?

It took all of Cici's will power not to backpedal. Instead, she just acted like everything she said was completely normal.

But thankfully, Baz didn't react like she'd said something wrong. He just huffed a sad sort of chuckle.

"I'm not so sure that's true but thank you."

Cici wanted to object to that on principle, but then Mama Gamal was entering with a steaming platter of food, and it was mealtime. After a simple prayer, Cici was more than happy to dig in. Maybe if she ate enough of Mrs. Gamal's cooking, she could gain a little weight.

Unlikely, though. Back when she was younger she wanted to be as muscular and built as Charity, but no matter how much she ate or worked out, she never migrated much past beanpole. It *had* gotten better in college, but she still felt so... so...

Skinny. Like the toothpick they teased her about in school.

Millers weren't small. They were tall with big personalities, intense eyes and impeccable character. Cici had maybe one of those traits on a good day. She was just so different from everyone else in her family. Except for maybe Benji, but even he was a towering human with plenty of svelte muscle.

Sigh.

But with Sabra, Baz and their parents, she never felt small. She never felt like someone apart. And it wasn't like she felt that way with her family either, but it was… well, it was different. It was just different.

It wasn't hard to fall into the lovely, boisterous conversation of dinner. While Mr. Gamal didn't cry when Sabra recounted her fitting, Mrs. Gamal did, and even excused herself at one point to 'check on the pie'. There was no pie, of course, but no one thought to refute it.

It was sweet, in a wonderfully loving way, and Cici counted each and every blessing the people around her had brought into her life through the years.

Like always, the meal went well beyond the eating of food, until all their plates were long since sitting empty. It wasn't until it was well past dark, and Sabra let out a particularly egregious yawn until they declared the dinner over, and even then there was the lengthy process of goodbyes.

With another half hour or so slipping by, it was that much more surprising when Baz's voice called out to Cici just as she began to descend the porch stairs.

"Hey, wait up a minute."

"Did I forget something?"

For once Baz looked a bit uncertain. He was usually so steadfast and astute in whatever he did, she wasn't used to him being even remotely off center.

"No, nothing like that. I just wanted to uh, chat a bit before you ran off."

"Chat? You mean like we just spent three hours doing?"

He huffed another nervous sort of chuckle. "That's different.

That was family talk. You and I haven't actually caught up since that time I came over to pick up that miracle soup."

Cici was acutely aware of exactly how long it had been since the last time that they were alone together. "Yeah, time really is flying."

"It is. Sometimes I'm worried that it's all slipped by so fast that I'm gonna blink and be a fifty-year-old bachelor who goes home alone every night and yells at young people to stay off his lawn. Or worse, living in my parent's basement."

Oh.

That was certainly a lot of unexpected information.

Baz must have realized it, because his eyes went wide and he stumbled over his words a couple times before being able to get started again. "Whoa, sorry. Didn't mean to get dark there."

"No, it's fine. I know what you mean."

"Thanks, you've always been pretty in touch with your emotions."

"Is that what you want to call it?" Cici said dryly, thinking of some of the episodes she had throughout her younger years. "I would like to think of it as personally terrorized by my emotions."

"Okay, fair on that one, but come on. It wasn't all bad."

Cici finally turned to fully face Baz. She'd been watching him out of her peripheral vision, like being at an angle to him would allow her to react like someone other than a schoolgirl with a crush.

"I distinctly recall being told you had to wrap me in a blanket and tackle me to the ground when I had a night terror and tried to fight something invisible down your stairs."

Baz just shrugged, as if that wasn't a big deal. "You had a lot going on as a kid, and I didn't mind. I can't imagine going through what you went through."

"Really? You didn't think I was a mess? Or find my outbursts..." she searched for the right words. She'd been given so many *words* about what she was throughout the years. Attention seeking, over dramatic, ridiculous, unsettling, off-putting, intense... They all ticked through her mind one after the other.

While Cici's family had been nothing but loving, kind and supportive, other folks were not. At least not after a while. Apparently, they thought it was strange that Cici would still be so virulently affected by her mother's death years after the fact. That she should be over the waking screaming in the middle of the night, of the sudden and unpredictable onset of intense panic attacks that left her shaky and breathless.

Cici hoped none of them had to experience just how life-altering losing a beloved mother was.

"Hey, they weren't 'outbursts'. You were sick. It wasn't like you were throwing a temper tantrum or anything."

Although Cici had been told those words many times and had largely dealt with the guilt she felt over how intense her needs were growing up, it was still definitely a balm to hear Baz say as much. Although she loved their family dearly, from time to time she couldn't help but wonder if they saw her as a burden. Some rich, mentally distraught girl that they had to be paid to want around.

Thankfully those times were few and far between, especially when she was seeing her therapist on a regular schedule.

"Some people aren't able to make that distinction."

"Well some people are idiots," Baz responded almost fiercely, as if he were defending Cici from the handful of people throughout her life who had been dismissive of her grief. Of her trauma. "But that's not news, is it?"

"Nope, definitely not."

He let out a little sigh and Cici couldn't help but wonder what was on his mind, what was on his heart. He seemed both troubled and freed in a strange, conflicting jumble of variables. Some moments she would catch him staring wistfully into nothing, as if he was longing for something he knew he couldn't have, and others he seemed so deeply intrenched in the present and enjoying life moment by moment.

"You alright, friend?" Cici asked, taking a step closer to him. Sure, she had plenty of complicated, unrequited feelings towards Baz, but he was her friend first and foremost. She cared about how he was and if he was okay.

"Yeah, I'm fine. Just thinking about time, and how sometimes it goes so quickly that you don't even know it's gone. Seems like just last year you and Sabra were preteens pretending to be pirates in the junk pile at your place."

"I remember that," Cici murmured, feeling a honeyed wave of nostalgia wash over her. They had just had the entire kitchen redone but due to an error in scheduling, the dumpster with all the debris wasn't picked up until a week after the project had finished. It had been the perfect spot to have 'buried treasure', and both she and Sabra had definitely clambered around it far more than they should have. "I can't count how many times we betrayed each other or mutinied."

"Yeah, it was pretty impressive considering you had a cast of two."

"We were nothing if not creative."

"That's for sure. But at least, no matter how terrible the war was, the two of you would always be down to sit down and have a picnic together in the end."

"I mean, Papa makes a mean picnic basket."

"Yeah, I definitely miss those."

The conversation petered out as Cici sank into her recollections as well. Those had been more innocent times, certainly more fun, but they were also full of fear and uncertainty. Between the grand adventures and the incredible stories, Cici mostly remembered feeling overwhelmed. Like there was a shadow lurking around every corner that would snatch away her loved ones the same way that it had snatched away her mother. She remembered feeling like a mooreless buoy lost at sea with no control over where she was flung.

Maybe that was why she'd clung so hard to her fantasies, adventures and make believe. Because in them she did have control. She made the world and decided the story. And she knew at the end of the day the heroes would always win. Unlike the sickness that had stolen her mother far too soon, the bad guys in Cici's worlds were always defeated.

"You know, we should do that again sometime."

Cici jerked out of her thoughts, blinking at the handsome man. "Huh?"

"The picnic, not the pirate part. It would be nice."

"Uh, I'd have to check Sabra's schedule but-"

"Oh, um... that's not what I meant."

Time for more blinking as Cici stared at him. What else could he mean? "I don't follow?"

He let out another one of those self-depreciating, dry chuckles, shaking his head. "Man, I'm messing this up." Cici felt like her heart was going to explode as he paused to draw in a deep breath. Was he going to- no, he couldn't... *could he?*

"I was asking if you wanted to go on a picnic together."

Another pause, and goodness, if there wasn't a whole world of uncertainty, in that single beat of silence.

"Just the two of us."

11

Cecilia

Cici stared in the mirror, wondering if she was dreaming. She'd certainly had her fair share of vivid visions during the night and picturing herself going on a date with Baz had certainly featured more than once.

No, not a date. A *picnic.* Thrilling, but not quite the same as a real, honest-to-God date.

Still, Cici couldn't help but wonder what was motivating Baz. Was he just trying to reconnect as friends? To catch up on all the lost time since she'd gone to college. Was he in some strange, just-past-quarter-life crisis?

She didn't know. And it wasn't like she could ask him either. Once he'd clarified that he was asking her, and specifically only her to a cute little afternoon jaunt, her brain had basically gone offline. She was lucky she'd even been able to accept the invitation and not helplessly babble incoherent gibberish.

And now it was almost time for their picnic, and she was only mildly freaking out.

Well, maybe a little more than *mildly* freaking out, but she had a handle on it.

Well, maybe not a *good* handle on it, but she was managing to hold herself together, so at least there was that.

"Breathe in, hold it for seven. Breathe out, hold it for seven."

That helped root her to the world. She hadn't had a panic attack in about seven months and she wanted to keep that streak alive. Besides, she didn't want Baz to feel like the thought of hanging out with him made her sick. Talk about sending the wrong message.

Not that she was trying to send a message, or anything. They were just two grown adult friends having a normal interaction. Just a nice, cozy, quiet little picnic.

It wasn't a date, Cici had to remind herself.

But it felt a lot like a date.

Her phone buzzed and a quick look at the text revealed that Baz was on his way. So she had maybe twenty minutes before he would arrive and she hadn't actually put on what she was planning on wearing. Which was pretty important for being in public.

"A skirt or a pair of pants? Or maybe shorts? Overalls?"

How casual was too casual? How dressy was too dressy? Cici didn't know and she was quickly running out of time. She supposed she could call Clara, but she knew her sister was helping Nathan with some of his animals and rebuilding his coop, so she felt like it would be pretty silly to interrupt all that just for some fashion advice.

Cici stared at her closet for another long moment before grabbing a pair of black leggings and switching out her top for a long button up that went almost down to her knees. That and a belt and she looked like a presentable human.

With another nod to her reflection, she hurried downstairs. No one was really about, which was certainly different than how it used to be, only three or so years ago. Back then, everyone was generally home no matter what the time was with only small exceptions every now and then. But more recently, Charity had Alejando and Savannah, which meant plenty of trips and events together that kept the eldest off the property more often. Cass usually shadowed Mickey, making a kind of franken-farmhand between the two of them. It was adorable, though. Charlie had the rodeo and Daisy, and even in the off season, they spent far more time together doing their own thing. And Clara had Nathan, spending equal times at his place as she did at home.

Even Papa, lovely, homebody, gardener Papa, had started to leave more often, spending time with that lovely librarian lady that he was sweet on. It was cute, and Cici really hoped that it went somewhere.

Papa deserved that much.

Actually, all of her family deserved happiness. They were such good people and they had been through so much. Cici owed her life to them about ten times over and she was never going to forget that.

So yeah, it was mostly just Cici around the house if she wasn't over at Sabra's.

And now it was going to be Cici and Baz.

Only Cici and Baz.

But it wasn't a date.

...even if it *really, really* felt like a date.

Rolling her eyes at herself. Cici rushed over to the fridge and, sure enough, the bottom shelf had a picnic basket sitting right there in the center. Pulling it out, she saw there was a note on the top written in Papa's sprawling sort of handwriting.

Knock 'em dead, sweetie.

Cici smiled to herself, her heart doing that thing it always did whenever her dad did something particularly kind. She really was blessed to have him in her life.

There was the sound of wheels across the driveway and Cici quickly grabbed the two thermoses that had been beside the basket.

It was time.

"Hey there, stranger," she said, opening her door while Baz was still heading up the porch. He flashed her that dazzling smile of his and for once, she managed not to be completely blinded.

"Hey there. Is that a basket I see in your hand?"

"I'm not sure how we'd have a picnic without it. Kind of a requirement."

"That and maybe a checkered blanket."

"I don't have a checkered one, but we do have a blue one that Clara and Cass made years ago. It's our designated picnic blanket."

"Oh wait! I think I remember that! Do you need me to grab it?"

"That'd be nice. My hands are full with the basket and drinks."

Baz nodded and followed her to the closet where the blanket was sitting on a shelf in one of their closets. With that in hand, they headed towards the pond on their property, slipping into conversation easily.

That was one of the things she always liked about him. Despite him being older than her, he was always so easy to talk to. And when he listened, it felt like he was really *listening,* which was practically a drug to young children with active imaginations.

"Oh man, this weather is beautiful. I'm so used to roasting at this time of year."

"Yeah, there's a storm front coming in tomorrow so it's a little cooler, and the breeze off the pond is nice."

"It is. How about this spot? Under the tree?"

"Works for me. The shade will be nice."

He nodded absently as he concentrated on spreading the blanket out, finding small rocks to weigh down each corner.

"There, a seat fit for a queen." He squinted at Cici, grinning mischievously. "Or are you a pirate today? A fairy?"

"I've just been Cici lately," she admitted, unable to stop herself from returning his grin in kind. "It's not as easy to access the magic that I could as a kid. Too much time spent in the real world, I think."

"It does kind of wear at you, doesn't it?"

"It does, but you can't let it get you down too much or you might miss out on the good things in life."

She managed to get a surprised look out of him and then he gave a comment she'd relish the rest of the night, "Like having picnics with old friends?"

The conversation continued to go back and forth naturally as they both sat and Cici began to spread out the contents of the basket. There were two small plates, cups and some cutlery along with all the cute little Tupperware containers. She saw deviled eggs, watermelon, hummus, chopped vegetables and then some cold cut sandwiches along with crackers and cheese.

Baz let out a whistle when she finished, looking over their small buffet. "I'm glad that my memory didn't exaggerate just how impressive these were. Did your Papa get a degree in perfect picnic packing?"

"While I appreciate the alliteration, I don't think that's actually a thing."

"It should be! I'm sure a lot of people would pay for this. I know I would."

"I'll make sure to pass on your compliments to Papa."

"Yeah, you better. I wouldn't want him to think I'm ungrateful and risk him never making me one of these again. That would be a true loss."

Cici shook her head, still chuckling at Baz's somber expression. She'd never really forgotten how funny he could be when he hit his stride, but it was making more and more sense why he was such a good babysitter when they were younger.

"Heaven forbid."

Naturally the conversation began to fade as they opened up the food and actually started eating, but they never quite sat in silence. Cici was grateful for the breaks that stuffing her mouth gave her, however. It gave her more time to think before she said anything and also for her brain to soak in everything Baz said.

It helped that the food was absolutely delicious.

But even truly scrumptious picnic fare couldn't stop her mind from churning through the same questions. Why had he asked her on the picnic? Did it mean anything? How could it mean anything? Was she looking too hard into it? Was she looking too little into it?

She could feel the panic building in her, insistent, demanding and vicious. The grass crumbled below her, opening up into an endless chasm that she didn't want to drop into.

And then Baz's phone rang.

"Huh, I thought I put that on silent. Lemme just check that real fast."

It wasn't much, but it was enough to knock her out of her spiral and she rushed to catch her breath while Baz talked on his phone.

"What do you mean?"

Uh-oh, that didn't sound good.

"Letter of intent? What does that mean? Really? I can't believe he took it that far."

"What's happening?" Cici asked, her curiosity perking up.

"Some rich guy ruined his car and is trying to sue our shop because of it."

"What, really?" Cici felt her anger rush up. If there was one thing she truly hated in the world, it was injustice. "You've gotta be kidding me!"

"No, I've got the other owner on the phone with me now and he just got served."

"Lemme talk to him."

"What?"

"Let. Me. Talk. To. Him."

Cici didn't have to use her firm voice very often, and clearly that strategy was working, because Baz's eyes widened, and he handed over the phone without an objection.

"Hello, this is Cecilia Miller, I'm a friend of Baz's."

An older but steady voice answered and Cici had to commend him on how smoothly he reacted to her intrusion. "Hello, Miss Miller."

"I hope you don't mind but I wanted to talk to you because my friend told me you're facing possible litigation."

"Yes. This isn't the first time it's happened, but it's been a while since I've had to deal with this."

"If you want, I can connect you with our family lawyer. He's prepaid and always willing to help."

"We do have a lawyer of our own."

"You do? Excellent!" Cici paused for a moment, debating what to do. "It's just that, our lawyer is really good. If you do a quick google search of his name, William Taylor, you'll see the kind of experience he has. Plus, he works with a whole legal team to help get the ball rolling."

"Legal team...?" Cici could faintly hear the sound of him typing and then a very pregnant pause. "Actually, I'd love to speak to your legal team."

"Fantastic. I'll text you the info, I have it pinned in my email account. You have a fantastic day Mr...?"

"Baxtin."

"Mr. Baxtin. Right."

"You have a good day too Miss Miller."

Feeling a little more like things were right in the world, Cici hung up and handed Baz the phone. But then she caught his expression, wide eyed and mouth slightly agape, and she suddenly realized exactly what she had done.

"U-um... sorry if I overstepped. I get really heated when people abuse their wealth or power."

Had she really just taken his phone and told his co-owner to search her family lawyer over the internet? She hoped Baz wouldn't be upset.

"You don't have to be sorry at all," Baz said, a slow and steady grin spreading across his face. "That was one of the most impressive things I've ever seen."

Oh.

12

———————

Baz

Cici was fully intrenched in his head and it seemed that she was there to stay. Everything about her just stacked up on top of each other, one right after the other, until it felt like his brain had an entire section dedicated to her and only her.

He didn't miss how she brightened his family's home whenever she visited. It was *impossible* to miss just how much happiness she brought to his sister. There was her easy laugh and her wit was as quick as anything.

And then there was how strong and determined she'd been when talking to Mr. Baxtin. There had been a fire in her eyes, a fierce sort of intensity and it was all for *him*. She was mad because someone was mistreating *him*.

She didn't tell him that he was being overdramatic, or even

tell him that it would all get better. She affirmed that someone was mistreating him and then she *did* something about it.

And boy did she do something. True to her word, the lawyer did get involved and last Baz heard, her legal team sent Moneybags a scathing letter that lined out what harassment and defamation were and that they'd be more than happy to pursue litigation to the full extent of the law.

So far, they hadn't heard back from the guy or his own questionable lawyer.

And with that weight lifted, things kept improving and the wedding kept marching ever closer.

Which, of course, meant hanging around Cici Miller even more.

And he certainly wasn't complaining.

He couldn't say when things began to switch more in his head regarding the youngest Miller. When she'd gone from the tiny little girl who was almost too fragile to live to a fully-fledged woman with an impressive backbone. Had it been when he'd first gone to pick up the soup? In those little flashes of meetings when she was over at his house? Hard to say. But what wasn't hard to say was that he was aware of her in a way that he'd never been before.

In a way that he probably shouldn't be.

How long had he and Victoria even been broken up? Not even six months. It was far too soon to be interested in someone and pretty inappropriate to be interested in his little sister's best friend.

But then he'd gone and asked her on a picnic. He couldn't say why he'd done it. He knew it was strange. But when she'd been standing there on his porch, quietly reminiscing with him about softer times, sweeter times, he'd suddenly been full of longing for that simplicity.

And the picnic had been lovely, it really had. Light. Airy. But with a touch of possibility and maybe even a strange sort of tension. It had made Baz feel so alive. So in the moment.

Then Moneybags had to go on and ruin the moment.

Man, that guy was really working out to be annoying.

"What are you moping about over there?" Sabra called, entering the kitchen with her arms full of snacks.

Baz looked up from where he'd been staring particularly hard at the microwave, popcorn still in hand. "Uh, just wondering if Cici will judge us for not doing this on the stove."

"Eh, Cici's pretty easy going. She'll probably just be glad that you're joining us for movie night!"

"It wasn't like I had anything else going."

"True, your life is pretty pathetic."

At that he turned to shoot Sabra a patented big brother look but she just stuck out her tongue. "Just because you're right, doesn't mean you have to say it."

"What can I say? I'm just a paragon of truth."

"Uh-huh, that's one way to put it."

At that she snorted and playfully batted his shoulder. "I'm glad to have you around more. It's making me a bit less anxious about my big day."

"Pre-wedding jitters are normal, but I'm here for you, no matter what."

She smiled softly, leaning her head against his arm. "As far as big brothers go, you're pretty awesome."

"Glad you think so."

Deciding to just put the popcorn in the microwave, Baz went

about the rest of setting up. He didn't know what a planning-session-and-movie-night was outside of it's name, but when he heard it was another chance to hang out with Cici, he jumped on it.

Maybe he should have thought twice about the fact that they would be interacting right in front of his sister, but oh well. Beggars couldn't be choosers.

"Oh! She just texted me that she's here!"

Phone in hand, she rushed over to the door and Baz took the tiny moment to look in the mirror hanging over their shoe rack and make sure there wasn't anything amiss about his appearance. No broccoli in his teeth, hair alright... yeah, it was as good as he was going to get.

"Hey there! I brought the movies!"

Baz turned and expected her arms to be full of DVDs, but instead she was holding a small, black little thing and a cord.

"What is that?"

"It's my portable drive, of course. I've got everything on here."

"You do know we have multiple streaming services, right?" Sabra prodded, shutting the door behind her friend.

"And do those streaming services have all the movies I love?"

"All the weird movies you love? Statistically, I would guess no."

"Well, I do. So clearly, my drive is superior to those streaming services."

Baz had to chuckle at that. Plenty of people who didn't know the two might think the two women were sniping at each other, but he was well used to their particular brand of banter.

"Alright, Miss Superior. You go plug it in and I'll grab our drinks. You thirsty?"

"Definitely." At that Sabra stepped out of the way and Cici's eyes landed on Baz for the first time. He found himself studying her expression intensely, noticing how her eyes rounded when she saw him and her cheeks flushed ever so slightly.

Interesting.

"Oh, Baz! Hi!"

"Hey, Cici. I hope you don't mind me crashing your movie night."

"N-no, not at all. You sure you wanna hang out with us little folk?"

"I don't know if I'd say either of you are very little anymore. I just want to hang out with the people who are important to me."

Nope, he wasn't imagining it. Her cheeks definitely flushed pink, and she licked her lips. He'd known her for over a decade and had never seen her lick her lips whenever she was nervous.

Very interesting.

"Wow, w-warn a lady before you hit her with wholesome content like that."

"I'll do my best."

She gave an awkward little nod that was way cuter than it had any right to be, then hurried over to the television. While she busied herself with that, Baz took the time to silence his phone and throw it on the charger. He wasn't going to give Moneybags or anybody else the opportunity to interrupt what little quality time he had with his sister and Cici.

Because he wasn't an idiot. He knew that once Sabra was married, she'd be caught up in being a newlywed. And he wanted that for her, but he also wanted to hog her as much as he could beforehand.

It seemed just yesterday he'd been clapping in their school's auditorium as she graduated from twelfth grade. And now she was about to start her own branch of the family.

Incredible.

Despite the tear in his heart, despite the complete and utter betrayal by his friend and Victoria, Baz hoped that maybe one day he could have that too. Someone who he could trust implicitly and who only wanted the best for him. Someone he could love, cherish, spoil and take care of. And someone who would, in kind, support and cherish him.

...and maybe that someone was kneeling in front of his TV, muttering something about USB cables.

...or maybe Baz was getting a little ahead of himself.

Yeah, definitely that second one.

But putting the horse ahead of the cart or not, it didn't take them long to settle in for the movie. Subtitles on, calendar in Cici's lap and binder in Sabra's, while the volume was on low, Baz was introduced to what planning and movie watching entailed.

And yet he didn't mind that he couldn't really hear the movie half the time. He also didn't mind that he didn't have a ton to contribute. Instead, he listened and ate delicious snacks, pitching in whenever his opinion was asked.

It was... nice. Simple. He'd forgotten what it was like to just sit down and *be*. To enjoy. He felt even more relaxed than he had in ages, and it was easy to imagine a long life just like this.

Except... except for his dream. Despite what happened with Red and Victoria, he *did* love working as a mechanic. And owning a shop. One day he wanted to have one in his own name and bring up his children in the business if they were so inclined.

But he'd never be able to do that on his own in their small town. He just didn't have the money or the connections. And even if he did, he wasn't likely to try that anytime soon. Especially not with taking a three-month sabbatical and bleeding through his savings while he recovered from his world being turned upside down.

The conflict churning inside of his brain was almost enough to knock him out of the peaceful contentment he'd been feeling with the whole situation, but then Cici pushed a bowl of chips into his chest.

"Hey, you okay over there?"

"Peachy," he responded, pretty pleased at how quickly he recovered. "Just debating the moralistic difference between taupe and beige."

"Hilarious," Sabra said, rolling her eyes as she set down the taquitos that Cici had brought. "I'm headed to the bathroom before you can come up with anymore zingers."

"You're missing comedy gold," Baz called after her, and she let out an unbelievable snort as she ascended the stairs.

Leaving Baz completely alone with Cici.

"Could you pause the movie for me? Sabra always forgets to and then comes back and has to rewind back to where we were."

"And she can never quite remember where we left off," Baz agreed with a laugh as he grabbed the remote and stopped the movie. The two were hardly even watching it, but he still understood not wanting to miss a whole chunk.

"But then she argues with you about it for a solid minute or two."

"A minute? Try five."

"Not with me. She actually likes me."

"I'm pretty sure there's a saying about blood being thicker than water that applies here."

"Actually, the phrase is 'The blood of the covenant is thicker than the water of the womb', but when people shorten it, they lose the original meaning."

"Only you would know that."

"I take that as a compliment."

They zinged off of each other without missing a beat, just a steady flow of snappy dialogue one right after the other. But it wasn't hurried or forced either. No, Baz definitely felt just as relaxed as he had a few moments ago.

Cici really was something. And by something, he meant an incredible person. Suddenly it was very urgent that she know just how amazing she was, and how much he appreciated her.

"Hey Cici, you—"

And then a knock sounded at the door.

"Huh? It's nine o' clock at night. Who do you have coming over this late who actually has to knock?" Cici asked, completely cutting off whatever ill-thought out thing he had been about to say.

"I... I have no idea."

The knock sounded again and Baz cautiously got up. They lived in a small enough town that it wasn't unheard of for a neighbor to pop by and ask for something, but it was unusual for it to be so late.

"I'll check it out."

Slowly, Baz headed over to the door and looked through the peephole. He wasn't sure what he was expecting, but it certainly wasn't platinum blond hair and a pale face he absolutely recognized.

"Oh crap," he breathed, heart stilling in his chest.

"What?" Cici called from the couch. "Who is it? Is everything okay?"

Baz didn't answer her. Instead, he opened the door to fully reveal the woman standing on the other side.

"Hey there, Bazzy-bear," Victoria said, stepping through the doorway like she belonged there. "Did you miss me?"

13

Cecilia

Life was feeling miserable.

Everything was bad, terrible, awful and otherwise malodorous.

Ugh.

Sure, she'd known that it was borderline impossible that anything would ever actually happen between her and Baz, but sometimes... it felt like it was _maybe_ going somewhere.

It was between his light touches every now and then, or the intensity of his eyes as he stared at her when he thought she wasn't looking. Or the kind things he said, or the picnic, or... or...

But then his ex had showed up and all of that ended.

How could she be so _naïve!?_

She knew better. Victoria was supposed to be the love of Baz's life. How could she ever hold a candle?

She couldn't. Point blank.

And if that weren't enough, Dani and her husband had returned back home while Charity was still doing finishing work on the interior of her future home, leaving Cici with three less people to distract herself with. Not that she could blame Charity for keeping busy. Her wedding date was supposed to be about four months after the house was finished, so it made sense for her to want to hurry it along.

So yeah, Cici did her chores everyday, helped Sabra when she asked, but for the most part moped, pined and otherwise pouted.

"Come on, Annabelle! How could you choose Marcus when it's so clear that Ferdinand has loved you forever?"

Oh, and yelled at whatever romantic plot was in the movie she was watching. The actors never answered back, however, and continued to make whatever poor choices she was trying to warn them against.

A knock sounded at her door and Cici had to fight her first instinct to throw her half-empty ice cream container at it. The last time someone had knocked unannounced at a door it had been an awful surprise, so she wasn't exactly eager to repeat the experience.

"Cici, it's me, Cass. I'm coming in."

Before she could object, the second eldest Miller opened the door, cane in hand and a stern look on her face.

"Go away, Cass."

"No."

"No? You don't get to tell me no! This is my room!"

"More like your own personal pigsty. Come on, Cici, let's get you up and out of here."

"I don't want to be up and out of here!"

"Yes, you do. You're just stuck in this cloud of misery and *think* that you don't want to. You think I don't know how depression works?"

A memory from not too long ago rose in Cici's mind, crisp within her recollection. Of Cass, withering in her own bed and angry, throwing things at Cici as she lugged a TV into her injured sister's room and insisted on some bonding time.

Yeah, if anyone got it, it was Cass.

"...what do you have in mind?"

Cass's face softened. "Mostly busy work. I was thinking cleaning Charity's tools, sanding off the new roof on the shed, maybe some weeding in the garden. Might even bake a cake for Clara. Figured that'd be a nice surprise."

Part of Cici wanted to say no. To tell her sister where to shove it and to stop being such a busy body. But the non-petulant side of her realized that really, she *did* want to get out of her slump. She hated soaking in her own pitifulness. That wasn't the Cecilia that she'd grown up to be.

"Okay. Let me just take a shower and I'll be right out."

"Fantastic. I'll see you in a bit." Cass went to turn on her heel, but paused, giving the room another look over. "On second thought, why don't I grab a trash bag and pick all this up while you're washing?"

"You don't have to do that. It's my mess, I can clean it up."

"I know I don't have to, but I'll do it anyways."

Cici couldn't argue with that. It was the same line she'd used on Cass before. It had been her turn to care for her sister then, and now it was Cass's turn to help her. Cici loved that about her family.

She'd never be able to survive without them.

Wiping her hands on her gross pajamas, Cici managed to

clamber out of bed and get herself into the shower. It was nice, having the hot water run over her and wash away the dirt along with everything else that felt like it was clinging to her.

Feeling a bit like a new woman when she got out, she went downstairs where, sure enough, Cass was waiting for her.

"You ready?"

"Yeah, let's be productive before I change my mind."

"Sounds good to me."

Together, they went outside where Cass's special cart was already waiting. Cici wondered if Mickey had dropped it off at the house for her then left to give them privacy. That was sweet. The two were pretty inseparable during their work week.

Cass was mobile and physical therapy had done wonders for her, but the uneven ground of the ranch always posed a little bit of a threat. It had taken a while, but Charity had managed to put together a custom electric chair-kart hybrid so Cass could pretty much go anywhere she wanted to go without worrying about twisting her ankle or losing her balance.

It also made the woman hard to keep up with, with her pedal-to-the-metal driving style.

"Hey, my legs are only so long!" Cici called after her when her older sister showed no signs of slowing down.

"Not my problem, slowpoke!" Cass called back, cackling the whole while.

"You're lucky it's in poor taste to hit an injured person!"

"You're welcome to try!"

Cici knew better than that. While she was fast and slim, Cass's biceps had always been impressive and the time in her wheelchair just made them that much bigger. She could probably pack a punch even if her body wasn't the same after her catastrophic injury.

"No thank you!"

Besides, it wasn't like they'd actually hit each other. That just wasn't their style. Sure, they'd rough housed from time to time as kids, mostly in water while playing chicken, but they'd never been very physically violent with each other.

As it were, it took Cici about three minutes after Cass to reach Charity's workshop, which felt strangely empty without the eldest Miller there. Without any fanfare, Cass started sorting, handing things to Cici occasionally and telling her either where to put it or how to clean it. Not too much later, Mickey showed up, arms laden with sparkling juice, fancy cheeses and what looked like a charcuterie board. Cici sent her sister a curious look, but Cass just shrugged.

"Figured if we were going to have a productive day, we might as well make an event out of it."

"Have I ever told you how much I love you?"

"You have. But I don't mind hearing it again."

"You know," Mickey cut in. "All the TV I watched told me that having siblings is way more tumultuous than this."

"Oh, our family is tumultuous, alright," Cass said dryly. "But instead of getting into fights and stealing each other's shirts, we lose our mother and get into catastrophic car wrecks."

"Or get blackmailed by our ex."

"Or assaulted in college."

"You both have a point and man, when you lay it out like that, I think I'd rather take the fights and stealing my clothing."

Cass snickered at that. "You would look a dream in Clara's fuzzy pink sweater."

But Mickey, ever the chill man that Cici took him to be, just rolled with it. "You think I could fill it out proper?"

"You could certainly try."

The conversation dissolved into laughter and then they moved on. And by moved on, Cici set up the food while Cass and Mickey continued to work.

Although work was a generous way to put it. It definitely felt more like hanging out and crafting rather than an actual job. And that feeling only increased as more family members filtered in and out of the workshop.

"Oy, is that a charcuterie board I see?" Daisy said, their first visitor to pop by. "I thought I smelled fancy cheeses."

"I would say something about that being impossible, but you can smell the difference between chocolates in a specialty box and that's basically unheard of," Cass said, holding out the cheese platter.

"Wait," Cici said, eyes wide. "You can do that?"

But Daisy just shrugged, going straight for the platter. "Yeah, apparently. Didn't know it was that unusual."

"Well, if you're going to chow down on cheese, how about putting these wrenches in their proper place in the red case?"

"Sure! Best payment I've ever heard of."

Cici was pretty sure that the whole world would be a better place if more people were willing to take cheese as payment.

They fell into a rhythm again until Papa showed up, armed with a lawn chair and a vegetable platter he'd made from the garden harvest. While he didn't help with the tools, he did go through his large basket, carefully binding herbs together so they could be hung up to dry in the newly redone shed. It was nice to have his presence again, even if he wasn't as chatty as Daisy or Cici.

Before Cici knew it, Charity's workshop was right as rain and then they were moving on to the next task.

Granted, Cici wasn't really as much of a handyman as the

rest of her siblings, so she mostly ended up watching and spraying the hose whenever it was needed while Charlie, Papa and Mickey took care of the roof. Cici could tell that Cass was chomping at the bit, wanting to be up there like she would've been before her accident, so Cici did her best to distract her as well.

Instead of being a mire of misery, regret and malfunction, it actually turned out to be a pretty good -and *tiring*- day. The next thing Cici knew, she was sitting at a delicious meal with a good number of her family, laughing, eating food, and forgetting entirely about the man who had unintentionally broken her heart.

There was only one downside to such distraction, however, which was that they always eventually had to end. Even with Cici sticking around to pick up the whole table and load up the whole dishwasher, that sinking feeling began to creep in on her the moment she was alone.

Drat.

"Breathe in, breathe out. Find the moment, find your center."

She repeated one of her many coping mantras to herself while inhaling and exhaling slowly. Maybe they sounded silly to anybody else, but they helped her when the panic or darkness were a bit too grabby.

"Hey, Cici, come finish this strawberry-basil lemonade with me."

Cici nearly jumped out of her skin, not realizing that Charlie was even around. "Coming!"

The sun was setting as she went onto the porch where her brother was sitting. Rays of sunlight shone up towards heaven through the vibrant pinks and purples of the sunset. It was beautiful in ways that only nights on the ranch could be, and Cici felt that anchor of peace nestle inside of her.

"Where's Daisy?" she asked, going to sit next to her brother as he rocked on the porch swing.

"She's off celebrating one of her friend's birthday parties. It was a bit too much social interaction for me, but she promised me that they're a group that watches out for her sobriety, so she feels safe going with them."

"That's awesome. I'm glad she has a good core group of friends."

"Me too. That's a treasure if I've ever seen one."

When Cici first met Daisy, she thought that maybe the charisma of Charlie would clash with the spotlight-grabbing gregariousness of Daisy. After all, there was only so much room in the spotlight. But no, the two balanced each other out and seemed to have an understanding that not every couple had.

"So, ya gonna tell me what has you down?"

"Pardon?" Cici deflected as he poured her a glass of the tasty drink.

"That time of the month is coming for Daisy in a few days, so I went to town to buy her favorite ice cream, but when I went to the freezer, half of our usual stash was gone."

"That obvious, huh?"

"Yuuuup."

"You know, most guys would be freaked out about a period."

"I grew up with four sisters. Besides, men who act weird about menstrual cycles are weak."

"Geez, no mercy from you."

"Never. Now stop trying to change the subject. What's got you burying your feelings in pints of ice cream?"

"I just... it's stupid. I'm acting like I'm in high school and honestly, I'm tired of myself."

"Like you're in high school? What, have you climbed a tree, forgotten you were in a tree, and then stepped out of a tree?"

"...that only happened once."

"Yeah, but the funny part is that it happened at all."

Cici couldn't help but grin at the memory. It had certainly been a lesson learned back in the day.

"So, if it's not falling out of trees, what's got you back in our glory days?"

"Ugh, please don't call them that. High school was the second worst time of my life."

"What was the worst time?"

"When Mama was dying."

Charlie let out a long breath. "I supposed I walked right into that one, didn't I?"

"At least a little bit." Cici could usually lead Charlie away from his point for hours, but that felt more than a little disrespectful considering how much he'd trusted the family when he'd shared with them the trauma he'd gone through in college.

Cici's heart ached every time she thought about it. And the idea that he'd kept it to himself for years because he'd been ashamed, because he thought that men couldn't be assaulted, made her want to wrap him up in warm blankets and give him hot cocoa until he forgot all the dark and dangerous parts of the world.

But, considering that Charlie probably wouldn't allow his little sister to swaddle him like a baby, perhaps just answering his question would be best.

"It's about Baz."

"Baz... Baz... I know that name..."

"It's Sabra's big brother."

"Oh right! I remember him. Me and him used to hang out occasionally when you were younger."

"Yeah, you tried to teach him how to ride a horse way back when."

"Keyword, tried."

"I think he's secretly intimidated by horses, but don't tell him that."

Charlie made a face. "I don't trust people who don't like horses."

Cici reached over and patted his thigh, sipping at her lemonade. "And you have the right to that opinion."

He snorted, and Cici couldn't help but grin cheekily at him. "Anyways, so what about Baz? He alright? Sick? Hurt? Suddenly turned into a jerk?"

"No, he's fine. Well, mostly fine. He's got a lot of tough stuff going on, which I supposed started all this but..." Cici wasn't trying to trail off, but she did, staring out over their family lands while lost in thought.

The truth was, she was more than a little embarrassed. In college she had prided herself on being independent, an excellent student, and a kind person. The thought that a man had taken over so much of her mind, mood and energy bothered her more than a little.

"But...?"

"You remember how I told you I was letting go of someone I loved who didn't love me back?"

"Yeah, I uh, I don't know if you know this, but that talk really stuck with me. It's what finally kicked me in the rear with Daisy. I almost lost her; you know."

Cici's eyes went wide at that. The idea of Charlie without

Daisy was like peanut butter without jelly. Sure, peanut butter was delicious and nutritious on it's own, but PBnJ was a next level deal that everyone loved.

Well, except for people who were allergic to it, but that was belaboring the metaphor.

"Wait, that talk with me is what sealed the deal for you?"

He nodded. "Yeah. I was very much in my feelings, and pretty confused by everything going on in my head, so I was pushing her away by doing nothing. My passivity was telling her that I didn't care, but in reality, I was scared."

"And you got over that fear?"

"I don't know if got over it is the right word. It's more like I acknowledged it and decided to keep going anyway."

"Wow. That's... that's amazing."

Although Cici had made great, great strides with her mental illness, she couldn't imagine just moving past her fear. It sometimes felt like panic and anxiety ruled so much of her life. Even when she had a relatively good handle on it, she still needed her therapy, her medicine, her coping mechanism and her support group

"And I owe it all to you."

"I... I don't even know what to say to that." Cici was so used to being the youngest, the one who came to her siblings for help. Not the other way around. Huh, the revelation was messing with her self-perception a little.

"How about you tell me why you brought it up since we both very clearly remember it."

"Well, I uh... I thought I let go of that love. I really did. I wished him well and decided to be happy that he found the love of his life."

"He? Is that he Baz?"

There was no use denying it. "Yeah. It was Baz. I think you're my only sibling that didn't know I had a crush on him the entire time we were growing up."

"Wait, you had a crush on a human mortal? I thought it would take elf ears and superpowers to make you fall in love with someone."

Cici chuckled ever so slightly at that. "Would it be cheesy to say that, when I was younger, it seemed like Baz absolutely had superpowers?"

"Since when do you care if something is cheesy or not?"

"Okay, you got me there."

"So, you were in love with Baz for years, but you decided to let that go because he found the love of his life, and the love of his life wasn't you."

"Basically."

"Your tone told me that things changed, however."

"Understatement of the year." Cici huffed, trying to put all of her thoughts in order. "You see, it was easy to be happy for him when he was off in the city and I only ever talked to him through a screen or text. And I *was* happy for him. I loved seeing him smile and there was this glint in his eyes whenever he looked at his girlfriend."

"But?"

"But then he came back. He was here, in our town, and he came into our kitchen. It was like my whole system was rocked. Suddenly I wasn't as over him as I had thought."

"I'm so sorry, Cici. That's... whew, that's a lot. Jealousy is a pretty intense emotion."

"I mean, yeah, but I could have dealt with jealousy if that was it. Like I said, I'm satisfied as long as he's living his best life. That's what I truly want for him."

"So if it's not jealousy, then what?"

"I found out that he and his girlfriend broke up."

"Wait, what?"

"And they broke up because she cheated on him."

"She *what?*"

"With his business partner and one of his long-term friends."

Charlie got up for a moment, pacing across the porch. The movement surprised Cici, but she let him walk away and come back without mentioning it.

"That's... that's awful, Cici."

"Yeah, it was. So suddenly, Baz wasn't happy. I wanted to comfort him. Protect him, you know?"

Charlie let out a breath and sat down beside Cici. "You know, I'm beginning to think that's a trait in our family."

"Thinking of everything that's happened in the past five years, I'd have to say you're absolutely right."

Despite how stressed she was, it felt good to share all the twisted stuff inside of her with Charlie. He was the second youngest, sure, but he was still older than her and she looked up to him. Besides, as her only brother, he had a unique male perspective that Cici didn't always think of.

"So, suddenly the love that you've given up isn't quite so unavailable as before, and you found yourself facing a whole lot of possibilities you didn't think would ever happen."

"Exactly."

"So I understand why that's an emotional rollercoaster, that doesn't quite explain the missing ice cream. He's single, little sis, if that's where your heart is leading you, go get it."

And there it was. The conversation had been going so well and Cici had been feeling positive about the situation, but then the whole reality of it came back. "I can't."

"What? Why can't you? Under a curse or something?"

"I wish it was something like that. Curses can always be broken, and the good guys win in those stories." Cici heaved a heady sigh. One deep enough that it almost made her lightheaded.

"So, what is it then? What's got you all tied up?"

"She came back."

"I'm sorry, what?"

"She came back while we were having a wedding planning and movie night. Just marched right into his parent's house like she owned it."

"You have got to be kidding me."

"I am one hundred percent serious. And he's basically disappeared since. Sabra's ticked off, of course. And I'm not pleased either. But I'm not sure if I'm unhappy because she hurt him and is waltzing back into his life like she didn't do anything wrong, or if I'm unhappy because what little chance I thought I might have is gone."

"Why can't it be both?"

That was enough to knock Cici out of her growing tirade. "Huh?"

"You can be mad that this woman broke your friend's heart without consequences and also mad that she ruined the little seedling of a chance you might have had with him. We humans are complex; it's not like things like this are in black and white."

"Oh."

"You didn't think about that possibility, did you..."

Cici felt her face heat. "... I guess not."

"What was that you said your therapist was trying to teach you? That boiling things down to unnecessary dichotomies doesn't solve anything and makes situations that much more stressful?"

"What, are you seeing my doctor behind my back?"

"No, believe it or not, I actually listen to you every once in a great while."

"Fake news. I don't believe it."

Charlie rolled his eyes but slung his arm over Cici's shoulder in a classic big brother side-hug. "Look, as fun as this banter is, I'm gonna remind you of something you once told me."

"And what's that?"

"You told me that the next time you felt so strongly for someone again, you'd fight for them."

Did I say that?"

"You did. That you would do whatever it takes, and you wouldn't expect things to just happen for you, even if you really, *really* wanted them to."

Cici didn't say anything, mostly because she didn't know what to say. She'd forgotten about that latter half of the conversation with Charlie.

But she had made that promise, hadn't she? That she wouldn't just wait for things to fall into her lap because she was too anxious or defeated to chase them herself and risk failure.

"So tell me, Cecilia Miller, are you gonna lay down and let this woman run rampant in your love's life without consequence," Charlie asked, voice much more serious than it had been for a majority of the conversation. "Or are you going to fight for him?"

14

Baz

To say Baz was conflicted would be a grave understatement to just about everything in his life.

Victoria had broken his heart. With her infidelity, she'd destroyed everything that they'd built up together. All of their memories were tainted, and their future dreams turned to dust. All of it, gone in an instant.

He loathed and resented her. He didn't want to look at Victoria or anything that was related to her.

But he also still loved her.

...or did he?

It was hard for him to sort it all out. He felt betrayed down to his very core, but Victoria had been the woman he'd imagined marrying and having a family with for years. It had only been two weeks past their third-year anniversary when he found out that she was being unfaithful, after all. That was over thirty-six months of knowing where his life was going only to have it suddenly yanked away from him.

But the real kicker, the salt rubbed into the wound, was that he wasn't even the one to end their relationship.

He was hurt, of course. It felt like someone had yanked out his heart. But he hadn't been willing to give up on everything they had dreamed about over the years.

So, he'd suggested couple counseling as a last-ditch effort to save their relationship and move on. He was willing to work through it.

But Victoria didn't want to.

She said things were easier with Red, that relationships shouldn't take so much work and that Red had more time for her. And then she'd walked out the door.

That was when Baz's world had closed in on him fully. When he'd contacted his landlord to end his lease and move back home with his parents until after his sister's wedding. When he'd gone on sabbatical from work so that he didn't have to see Red or anything that reminded him of Victoria.

And then, just when he felt like he was starting to recover, like he might be able to move on and find a new path in life, she'd shown up at his door, looking absolutely *incredible.*

He'd forgotten how breathtaking she was. From the sweet, softness of her round face to the honey-brown of her doe eyes. The long, elegant line of her neck before it faded into her graceful shoulders and generous frame. The dramatic curves of her body, which he knew were so soft and warm against him.

It was like being hit by a tornado of want, hatred, longing, and desire all at once. Baz couldn't really say exactly what had happened after she arrived, but he knew after a bit Sabra tersely escorted Victoria right back out and he went to bed.

Baz's phone buzzed and he pushed himself out from under his car. It didn't really need any work, but he needed to keep his hands busy with how full his mind was. Unsurprisingly, it was a text from Victoria.

I just wanted to say sorry again.

Baz just stared at the text, his mind going a million miles a minute. She'd said sorry when she'd come into his parent's house, but he'd been so shocked that he hadn't had a response. In truth, he still didn't have a response. Because what was there to say?

If she'd been apologetic from the beginning, maybe he wouldn't feel so cautious. But the way she'd stared at him as he cried to her, asking why she'd done it all, then walked out the door of their house, was burned into his memory like a painted picture.

I'd like to try that couple's therapy, if you're still open.

Baz's eyes were starting to burn from how hard he was staring at his phone. Words kept flying through his head, some bitter, some thrilled, some angry, but none of them seemed right.

Why did you do it?

No, that wouldn't get them anywhere, and honestly, he wasn't sure he was ready for that answer.

Do you really think you can walk right back into my life!?

No, that wasn't a good idea either, because he wasn't sure if she couldn't. Part of his heart and his mind was screaming for her, begging for a crumb of her affection. He was like a junkie succumbing to the need for another hit even though he knew it was terrible for him.

Yes. Please. Anything.

And that wasn't it either. He couldn't just let her walk all over him. Hadn't multiple people in his life told him how great it was that he was standing up for himself and setting boundaries? He couldn't betray that. He didn't want to betray that.

His thoughts were quickly growing overwhelming, so he got up and went to the kitchen for a drink. But even downing a cool, crisp draft brew didn't help him, so after some pacing, he looked at his phone again.

It seemed Victoria had been busy while he was pacing.

I want to prove that I've changed.

I was selfish.

I know I don't deserve a second chance, but I'm pleading with you for one. Please. I miss you.

He could practically hear her sweet, husky sort of voice as she said it. He remembered those same plush lips of hers pressed against his ear, whispering all sorts of sweet nothings and promises that would never come to be.

Hurt welled up in him. Bitter and vicious. But hope was right there with it. Daring to believe that maybe, just maybe, all of his dreams weren't ruined.

But there was one little hitch. Or perhaps not a little hitch. Every third thought or so, his mind clicked over to Cici all on its own.

Strange.

Actually, no, if he stopped being in denial for a minute, it wasn't that strange at all. Something had changed between him and the youngest Miller daughter. She wasn't some little daydreamer anymore. She was a hilarious, determined and fierce woman that he couldn't help but admire.

And he would be lying if he said he wasn't attracted to her.

He liked her strong features, with her cut cheekbones and intense Miller eyes. He liked the long, lithe lines of her body and how she skittered about whenever she was excited. She was the antithesis to Victoria in almost every way, shape and form, but Baz liked that. There was so much beauty in the world, after all, he didn't feel like he could only appreciate one form of it.

If you don't want to, I understand. But I really hope you'll give us a try.

I still love you.

Oh.

Oh no.

Those were words that he couldn't ignore. His fingers twitched as they hovered over his phone, needing to say something but unable to get any words to come out of the tips of his digits.

Why would you-

I can't really-

This isn't-

WHY!?-

How can you say that?

You're full-

One right after another, as soon as he typed something, he'd delete it. He was chasing himself in circles and making himself sick to his stomach.

Finally, he settled on it.

Can I call you?

There was no answer for a moment, and he had the alarming thought that he'd somehow fallen into some sort of trap. But then his phone buzzed again.

Of course. Anytime.

With one last deep breath, Baz hit her number and let the phone ring.

IT TOOK a week and a half to get into a couple's therapist, and that was way faster than Baz had expected.

"So, today we're not going to do any massive problem solving or anything like that," the therapist said. Baz had already forgotten her name, but she was a middle-aged woman with a no-nonsense sort of air to her. "Today you're both going to tell me why you're here, and what you hope to gain out of this. We're all going to be learning about each other and figuring out the best paths to accomplish all of our goals.

"And it's okay if you don't have any set goals. Not everyone comes to therapy because they need to fix something. Some people come because they want a reminder of why they love each other, or because they're struggling with other aspects of their life and are seeking support. You're not broken because you're here."

That actually made Baz feel better, and he cleared his throat. But before he could say a single word, Victoria was talking.

"We're here because I violated Baz's trust. I broke the promises we made to each other, purposefully broke boundaries and was incredibly selfish.

"But I've changed, and I want a chance to make it up to him. I also want the help to make sure that I never do anything like that again. Baz is the love of my life, and I hate myself every time I think that I've ruined our chances."

Whoa...

Baz's eyes widened and all of his words left him. He had

never expected Victoria to be so honest about what had happened or take responsibility for the crumbling of their relationship. He'd thought there would have been more blame slinging, or her trying to minimize what she'd done. But no, there it was, right out there in the open.

"Thank you, Victoria, for explaining all of that. It takes a lot of integrity to be honest when we've made bad decisions that hurt people."

"I'm sorry. I really am. If I could take it all back, I would, but I recognize that the real world doesn't work like that.

"But I am willing to put the time in, and whatever else is needed. I want to make this work, I really do."

Every single word out of her mouth made the small, hidden part of his heart that still harbored her grow a little bigger. Those dreams he had been mourning were beginning to resurrect, brushing dust off their metaphorical shoulders.

And there was something else growing inside of him. Something that might actually be forgiveness. He'd thought he could never forgive her, that the wounds she'd given him would scar him for life. But the soothing coolness of it washed over him ever so slightly, promising that maybe tomorrow could be better. That maybe not all was lost.

"And what about you, Baz? Do you want to make this work?"

Baz didn't answer right away, because he wanted to be as honest as possible. Did he want to make it work?

...did he?

He still loved Victoria, he knew that much, but he also knew that she'd hurt him terribly. And he also knew that their relationship wasn't the healthiest.

Was this a relationship worth fighting for?

"I... I believe so. But I want to make sure that we would be good for each other."

"That's good that you have that boundary, Baz. It shows that you care for both your health and Victoria's."

"You... you aren't sure that you want to be with me?" Victoria asked, voice tremulous.

It was now or never. He could be honest with her, or he could lie, and lying would ruin any chance they had together. "No, I'm not sure."

"...oh."

He hated hearing Victoria sound so small. She was such a gregarious person, full of personality and charisma. It wasn't like her to be uncertain.

"I'm sorry, Victoria. I loved you, and I love you still, but I refuse to let myself be hurt like that again. I've built these walls up to protect myself, and I don't know if I can tear them down so easily."

"I... I'm so sorry that I've hurt you. I hate that I did this to you."

"And I believe you. But you have to understand. I lost my best friend too. I trusted him. We've been ride or die since we met in high school and now he's gone. He won't even return my texts or apologize. It's great that you're willing to apologize, but that's only half the wound for me."

Victoria began to cry, and Baz's heart ached for her, it really did, but he had to tell the truth.

It wasn't the only wave that was rushing through him, however. There was still bitterness there. Still distrust. She had been so flippant in her betrayal that it was difficult for him to move past that.

Then again, it was just the very first day of couple's therapy. Who knew what the future appointments might hold?

15

———————

Cici's heart felt like it was going to explode as she marched right up to Sabra's home. Her breath was coming much quicker than it should have, but that was probably because she'd been holding it for way longer than was healthy while she was sitting in Charlie's jeep.

She still couldn't believe that a one-off conversation she'd had with him almost a year ago had changed the course of his life so much, and she especially couldn't believe that it was helping *her* now too.

She had said she'd fight for her next love. Well, it was time to throw down the gauntlet and put up a fight.

Her resolve wavered ever so slightly as she raised her hand to ring the doorbell. Then she stopped. What was she doing? Baz was her ex-babysitter and her best friend's brother. There was no way he'd ever be interested in her in that way!

But she clamped down on that with an iron fist. In truth, it didn't really matter if he felt that way towards her or not. What mattered was that Cici was straight forward and stood up for herself. That she stopped living a passive life and was proactive about things. Even if he said no, even if he gently turned her down, it was important that she fight for the things and people she valued.

So she rang the doorbell.

Was it louder than usual? It seemed like it was louder than it used to be. But before she could figure out if the volume had been turned up or not, Sabra opened the door.

"Um... you didn't call. Something up?" Sabra looked her up and down, and it was a testament to their friendship that understanding crossed her face within seconds. "You're on a mission, aren't you?"

Cici nodded, shifting the basket she was holding from one arm to the other.

"Yes, I am. May I speak to Baz, please?"

Anybody else would have asked questions, but not Sabra. Instead, she smiled a knowing sort of grin and spinned around on her heal.

"One Baz, coming right up."

With that she disappeared inwards, door still open, but Cici didn't follow her. She was being brave, she was fighting for the man she loved.

It didn't take long for Baz to return, and he too gave her a quizzical sort of look, not that she could blame him.

"Did I forget someone's birthday or something?"

"No, nothing like that." It wasn't too late. She could still just turn tale and go home so wouldn't have to stand there and experience Baz rejecting her. It would be so easy...

But she wasn't going to take the easy path. She was going to put up her dukes and fight.

"This is for you, actually." Without any flourish, she handed the basket over to him. It was a towering thing, full of gift cards, goodies that she and Clara baked together, some of Daisy's cheese recommendations, craft beers and a few drawings Cici thought he would like.

"...for me? Did I do something?"

"No. Yes, actually. Um..." *Get yourself together, Cici.* Steadying herself, she drew in a deep breath and tried again. "This is a courting gift. Because I'd like to court you."

Oh no, he was staring at her. He was staring at her like she'd grown another head and she felt like she was going to die.

"You what?"

"I like you. I've liked you for a long time. And if you're not interested, that's one hundred percent fine. I still want you to enjoy this basket and think about all the wonderful memories we've shared together.

"But if you have any shred of that sort of affection for me, then I'm declaring my intentions. Baz Gamal, I would like to formally court you."

She could see Sabra silently cheering behind his back, jumping around the kitchen and waving her arms in excitement. But Baz said nothing.

And continued to say nothing.

In fact, she was pretty sure he wasn't even blinking.

"Cici... I..."

This was it. When he was going to gently turn her down and she could admit defeat. It wasn't what she wanted, but at least she could proudly say that she really had tried. She hadn't just laid down and let her anxiety rule her.

"I just... You should know that I'm trying to work things out with my ex."

Oh, she knew. She was *keenly* aware of that.

"I figured as much, but I still wanted to make my intentions known. You have options, outside of her. I mean, you have options outside of me too, I just want to eliminate any doubts that I'm attracted to you, Baz, and I could see something good happening between us."

She couldn't believe she was doing it. She was in the home stretch! And what was insane was that the nerves were actually dwindling the more she spoke.

"Just remember, whatever you decide, I will one hundred percent respect your decision and I will always cherish your friendship." She managed a real, genuine smile. "Because we make pretty amazing friends, don't we?"

The smile he gave her was soft and ever so sweet. If they were in a movie, it would have been the moment that she stepped forward and they shared a passionate kiss. But life wasn't one of Clara's classic romance movies, so instead Cici took a single step back.

"You deserve great things, Baz. I hope you know that."

"...I'm beginning to think maybe I do."

That was one of the best things that he could have said. Sure, Cici wished that he'd throw himself into her arms and given her a kiss that lifted her feet off the ground, but hearing that Baz believed he was deserving of good things wasn't bad either. If he truly believed that, he most likely wouldn't let Victoria violate his boundaries again.

With one last nod, Cici gave a lil' salute and headed back to her jeep.

All she had to do now was wait.

16

———

They were in couple's counseling again, and Baz was so conflicted.

It would be so much easier if Victoria was just a villain. But she really did seem to be trying. She'd accepted responsibility for how her actions had hurt him and offered no excuses. It was refreshing, as much as it made his heart squeeze with pain every time he thought about her and Red together.

"So, Victoria, from what you've said, you were drawn to Red because you felt he was giving you what you were missing?"

"Yes. And I feel terrible for saying it, but I felt so neglected in our relationship, and then I felt terrible for feeling neglected."

She felt neglected? That was news to Baz.

"And why do you believe that you felt that way?"

"Because Baz worked so hard, and I realize that it was

because he was saving for our future, but I never got to see him. A lot of my work would happen at night or on the weekend, and Baz was working fifty to sixty hours in the shop, mostly during the day."

Oh... Baz did remember having a couple of conversations about that. Victoria saying she missed him, saying that she was lonely, and he'd tell her that he'd try to take more time off.

He never really got better though, did he? Not really. He was pretty sure he'd started spending even more time in the shop so he could surprise her with their Hawaiian vacation together.

But since it had been a surprise, he hadn't told her about it. And since he hadn't told Victoria *why* he was spending even more time in the shop after she asked him to do the opposite, could he really blame her for feeling neglected?

Obviously cheating was her choice, and 100% her responsibility, but Baz was beginning to wonder if he perhaps hadn't been the spectacular partner he'd always thought he was.

"Red paid attention to me. Made me feel like I was the most important thing in his life. At first I just waved it off as he was Baz's good friend and business partner, so he was just being nice, but it quickly became something... more."

"Something more?" the therapist prodded with an impressive amount of objectivity in her tone.

"Yeah. I tried to fight it, I did. But it all happened so fast."

Despite wanting to tell her that she was ridiculous, that feelings just didn't 'happen so fast', he couldn't help but think of Cici. Sure, he wasn't in love with her, not quite, but he couldn't deny that the connection they'd always had, had definitely shifted to something a little different than before.

"Baz, are you alright? You seem distracted."

"Huh?" How far had he drifted? He didn't even know. "Oh, yeah. I'm sorry. I guess I have a lot on my mind."

"Anything you'd like to share?"

His first instinct was to say no, but that would be a lie, wouldn't it? And if Baz wanted to give Victoria a fair chance, then he needed to be truthful.

"Actually, sure. I was asked out by someone and it's brought up some conflicting feelings."

"Oh, that's very interesting, Baz. And how do you feel about—"

"Excuse me, you *what!?*"

Victoria's enraged voice cut off the doctor and it was so loud and heated that Baz was taken completely aback.

"I, uh, there—"

"Are you *kidding* me? I'm here, prostrating myself across the ground for you, groveling for you, and you're thinking about somebody else!?"

"Victoria..."

"No, don't you 'Victoria', me! I can't believe you! How could you do this!?"

"I haven't done anything! I'm just being open and honest about something that happened. Do you want me to lie to you?"

"Pffft, open and honest, yeah right. I see what you're doing here!"

Anger shot up in him, but so did hurt. Why was she freaking out so much?

"Look, I don't need to sit here and be disrespected while you make up fake people who asked you out. You want me to be jealous? You want to paint me like some kind of monster? Well congrats, you did it!"

"I have no idea what you're talking about."

"Sure you don't. You always have to be so *good* and I'm always the bad guy. Whatever. I don't need this!"

Before Baz or the therapist could say anything, Victoria got up and grabbed her purse. She marched out and slammed the door so hard that one of the therapist's degrees fell off the wall.

Baz could hear her swearing the entire way down the hall until the elevator dinged. And then, once that faded, there was complete silence.

Perhaps unsurprisingly, it was their therapist who spoke first.

"That's not the first time that degree has fallen."

"...I don't know if that's supposed to comfort me or not."

"If you find comfort in it, then take it. I was simply stating a fact."

"Right."

Another few moments of absolute silence before she cleared her throat. "Would you like to schedule a session for another time?"

"Yeah, actually," Baz said slowly, realization beginning to click inside of him. "But not for couple's therapy."

"Oh?"

"I'd like to have some individual therapy. Just for myself and to work on all these wounds I've got from cheating and some other unhealthy habits I've developed."

"So no more couple's therapy?"

"You don't have to worry about that. There won't be anymore couple's therapy because Victoria and I are never going to be a couple again. Ever."

Cecilia

Cici stared up at the sky as she idly paddled, enjoying the very last of the sun before it set and enjoying a few of her sibling's company.

Granted, Daisy and Charlie were laying on a blanket together by the shore, napping, while Charity was helping Savannah try to back stroke. But Cici didn't have to be in direct conversation with them to feel happy in their presence, and she was able to just let herself drift.

She was more relaxed than she'd been in ages. Sure, she would have liked it if Baz could have given her any sort of answer in the week since she'd talked to him, but she also knew she couldn't rush it. Not if she really cared for him. Although it was certainly hard to resist the temptation when Sabra kept updating her on every little thing she observed about Baz and Victoria.

Ugh. Victoria.

Cici had never wanted to curse a woman so much, but she forced herself to contain her ire. Victoria had made a mistake, and if Baz wanted to forgive her... well, that was his business. She knew he wasn't stupid, so if he was willing to risk trusting her, he had to have a good reason.

...or he was just love sick.

No, she wasn't going to be critical of his choice to try. To get counseling. Even if it didn't work out between them, hopefully it would help heal the wounds that they'd clearly given each other.

So, with her trying valiantly to keep her heart in the right place, Cici had asked her best friend to chill on the flood of info. Unfortunately, not before she found out that Victoria hadn't come over to the house since and that Baz had only left a couple of times for couple's therapy.

Yeah, *couple's therapy*. That was wild. Cici's nerves definitely went all frazzly every time she thought about it, but she also was incredibly proud of him for going the extra step and trying to save a relationship he valued. Sure, it might not be exactly what she wanted, but it showed that Baz was setting boundaries for himself and demanding respect.

Which... made her happy.

"Always a silver lining," she mumbled to herself, grinning as she floated. She did feel so much more at peace now that her feelings were out in the open. There was so much less doubt and uncertainty. She no longer woke up dreading the day or addicted to the thought of what Baz was doing that day.

"Hey, did you remember your sunscreen?" she heard

Savannah call to her, splashing into the water and interrupting her reverie.

"Yeah, I put some on about forty minutes ago."

"Okay! I'll remind you in an hour!"

"You do that!"

Maybe to anybody else, the pre-teen's insistence would have been annoying, but to Cici, it was just another sign of how supported and loved she was. She remembered meeting the young girl when she was just eleven, and she'd had a feeling the girl would fit right in with their family. It turned out that she had been way more right than she knew, and now Savannah was set to become an actual in-law.

Now if only her feelings about Baz could be so accurate.

"None of that," she chided herself. "You are enjoying a lovely afternoon in the pond with your siblings. No moping. No pining. Period."

But all the self-admonishment in the world couldn't stop those little tendrils of doubting darkness from creeping into her mind. She needed a distraction and fast.

Maybe a sandwich?

"Why not, food fixes most things."

That did get a wry chuckle out of herself and she tried not to wonder what it meant that she laughed at her own jokes. Some things were never gonna change, and her being goofy was one of them. After all, years-long unrequited love or not, she was just Cici, finally, regular old Cici. It was...

Wait.

...was someone playing guitar?

Sitting up from her innertube, Cici shaded her eyes so she could look around. Charlie and Daisy were still napping, while

Charity, Savannah and Alejandro had moved onto the shore where they were all eating Italian ices from their coolers.

So where was the music coming from?

And then she finally saw it, Baz, riding up to her on a horse, playing a guitar she only vaguely recognized.

What was going on!?

Paddling towards the shore, Cici openly stared at the handsome man as he approached. She couldn't remember the last time she saw him on a horse; hadn't she just confided in Charlie that she was pretty sure he was afraid of them?

She was struck speechless by the whole thing, but that seemed to be alright, because Baz played the entire way, until the horse reached the edge of the pond. With that he dismounted and handed the guitar to Cass, who had rolled up behind him sometime when Cici was distracted.

"What is going on?" Cici asked, almost to the shore as well. But she couldn't quite close that distance between them, standing knee deep in the water like it was an entirely different world.

But Baz just grinned and reached into his backpack, pulling out an impressive bouquet of flowers that he brandished with plenty of flare.

"What's going on here, Miss Cici Miller, is that I'm asking you out on a date."

Wait.

What?

He *what!?*

If Cici wasn't acutely aware of her audience, she would have pinched herself. But as it were, she still couldn't help but sputter in her shock.

"Y-you came to ask me out with a h-horse and a serenade?"

"Well, I certainly couldn't be boring about it, now could I?"

Cici continued to stare at him like her mind was trying to analyze every single little detail for a trick or trap. Because Baz Gamal couldn't be asking her out. He was going to couple's therapy and trying to work things out with his ex!

"What about Victoria?"

While Cici wanted him, desperately so, she would never be the other woman. She knew she wouldn't be happy with and didn't deserve that situation.

"I promised to give her a second chance, and I did. We're just not healthy for each other."

"O-oh…"

So that was it. Baz Gamal was no longer a taken man and was interested in going on a date with her, Cici Miller.

Incredible.

"So, what do you say? Up for an adventure with me?"

Cici's heart practically leapt into her chest and she thought it might explode right then and there. She wasn't sure if she was laughing or crying, but she let out a squawk of a noise and rushed forward, arms extended.

Yet somehow Baz was right in step with her, rushing into the shallows of the pond despite his shoes and socks. He caught her, just as she hoped he would, and lifted her up, swinging her around like a scene out of a romance movie.

She wasn't going to lie, she'd always been a little jealous of her siblings when their loved ones did that, always wondering when it would be her day to make someone so happy that they had physically lift her towards the heavens to express it. She never thought she'd actually have the experience, yet that was exactly what was happening.

This time she knew it was laughter that bubbled out of her,

genuine, giddy laughter. It overflowed from her heart and mind, spreading all around them in a cloud of absolute bliss.

Time did that funny thing where it lost all meaning, and she couldn't say how long they stayed in each other's arms after the fact. But eventually, she was staring up into Baz's deep, chocolate eyes. Goodness, that was a beautiful pair of eyes.

"So, was that a yes?" he asked, grinning at her in that perfect way of his.

"Yes!" Cici declared unabashedly. Unapologetically. Whole-heartedly. "Yes, Baz, yes!"

"It's a date then."

Yes, it most certainly was.

18

———

Cecilia

 n the years since her siblings had started dating, Cici
had heard a lot of amazing stories *and* horror stories
about first dates. Some were in restaurants around town, some
were in the next city over, some were even in fields of fireflies.

But her and Baz's first date?

It was in his home with a meal he'd cooked himself. Which
was just perfect to her.

"I can't believe that you actually managed to get everyone out
of the house," she mused, chin in her hand as she watched him
put food on her plate. She liked that he wasn't one of those
weirdly macho guys who thought a woman's place was in the
kitchen. In fact, she was pretty sure that Baz was a better cook
than her. But considering how much Clara and Papa liked to

prepare meals for their whole family, it wasn't like she got too much practice.

"You'd be surprised, actually," Baz admitted, finishing her plate off with a triumphant flourish. Goodness, he was so cute. She loved that he was so unapologetically extra around her. It always felt like he was embracing her fantastical view of the world. "Once I told them why I needed the space, they were all more than happy to keep themselves busy.

"In fact, I'm pretty sure my parents are on their own date right now. They said it had been ages since they'd taken a night out on the town."

"Aww, that's so sweet!" Mr. and Mrs. Gamal were so blatantly in love and Cici never got tired of it. Although sometimes it made her feel a bit sad for Papa. Was that what he'd had with Mama? She could only imagine so. But what she couldn't imagine was what it was like to have that and then lose it suddenly.

Wait, no. She wasn't going to think about depressing things on her first date with Baz. It was something she'd wanted to happen for over a decade and she wouldn't allow herself to self-sabotage.

"Well hopefully you'll think it's even sweeter that I covered the whole night for them. They're gonna go see a movie at that huge theater in the city, then go out to a sushi place they've been eyeing for at least a year."

Gosh, he was so sweet. Cici loved how he liked to take care of everyone around him. Not because she needed to be taken care of, but because she knew how hard Baz worked for his money and yet he was still happy to spend it on those he loved.

"That's brilliant! I'm sure they're going to have a wonderful night."

"I hope so. And I hope we do too," he said as he pushed her plate towards her.

"Mmmm, judging by how this food smells, it's going to be a great night."

"Yeah, I like to make up for having a terrible personality by covering it up with good food."

"It must be working so far, because I think you have an amazing personality."

"Hah! Flatterer."

It happened in less than a second. One moment she was bantering with Baz, the next he leaned in and gave her a quick peck on the cheek.

Her body's reaction was instantaneous. There was a mini-explosion in her chest and it spread outward from there until her face was on fire and her toes were curling in her shoes.

Was *that* what it felt like to be kissed by someone she loved? What a feeling. Cici could see why all of her siblings got a little soft eyed and sappy whenever they talked about their partners.

Oh boy.

She wanted more.

But part of her shock must have shown in her expression, because Baz quickly straightened.

"Sorry, I suppose I should have asked for permission."

"No!" Cici objected, a bit too quickly and far too loudly. But Baz had the good sense not to tease her about it, allowing her to clear her throat and try again. "I mean, uh, consider permission granted."

"That's an awful lot of trust you're putting in me."

"Well, I trust you, so it makes sense."

It was a simple enough statement, but Baz ducked his head,

and she swore she saw his cheeks color too before he answered. "I suppose it does when you put it like that."

She could tell that he was trying to find a way out of their particular conversation path, no doubt flustered by her stark statement. But she didn't mind the little hint of awkwardness, they were awkward people after all. And she wanted Baz to know where she stood. She unequivocally trusted him, whether it was in the role of her friend or potentially... her boyfriend.

Was it silly that thinking that one particular word made her toes curl up in her shoes twice in one night? Probably, but she didn't care. She was on her date with Baz and she wasn't going to let a single thing dampen it.

"Soooo," she said, giving Baz the segue he was looking for. "Are you going to serve yourself or am I meant to eat on my own while you watch?"

"Serve myself?" His eyes landed on his empty plate still in front of him. "Oh! Right! I suppose that's important."

"Yeah, I hear that actually having food to eat is an important part of having a meal."

"I'm sure it took many scientific studies to prove such a thing."

"Oh yeah, dozens. Maybe even hundreds."

And just like that, they were back into the easy flow of things. After the shock and joy of him asking her out had worn off, Cici had been so sure that their date would be full of tension and stilted dialogue as they both tried to figure out where they stood and what was possible between them. But it turned out she had worried for nothing, because things were just as smooth as they'd always been.

Naturally it didn't hurt that the food was absolutely delicious, and just like the picnic, she found herself able to buy time for her thoughts by making sure her mouth was full.

But unlike the picnic, she wasn't full of panic. No, instead she was relaxed and content with maybe only a slight tinge of nerves.

"So," Baz said cautiously about halfway through their meal.

"So?"

"You've liked me for a while?"

She huffed a short laugh, but then realized he was being serious. 'Wait, you didn't know?"

"...should I have known?"

"Baz, everyone knew I had a crush on you growing up. Including your parents."

"You're kidding."

"I often do, but not about this."

No, not about that at all. Cici loved to be funny, that was true, but she wouldn't joke about that.

...at least not super often.

"I have no idea how I never knew. You weren't very obvious."

Cici let out a sound that was somewhere between a snort and a choke. "Um, I really, really was." She shook her head. "I guess it's a good thing you didn't notice, because I probably would have made you uncomfortable."

"I mean, I guess. I always thought it was creepy when college guys hit on high school girls."

"Oh yeah, it's definitely creepy. It's probably a good thing you didn't return my affections, I totally recognize that." Cici chewed her lip a moment, wondering if she should ask her question or not. But hey, she was being brave, wasn't she? She might as well ask.

"So... when did that change for you?"

"Huh?"

"Possibly returning my affections?"

"To be honest, I wasn't sure that you were into me at all until you said so."

At that Cici almost spit out her food, which would have been a shame because it really was delicious. "Are you serious?"

"Uh, yeah." There was that blush again. It was almost imperceptible against his deeply tanned skin, but Cici didn't miss it. "I mean, I think I know the moment where I started to see you as a grown up, as Cecilia Miller instead of little Cici, but I honestly had no idea you felt the same about me."

...wow.

Cici continued to stare at him for a long moment, completely taken aback. All these years she'd thought she'd been so obvious, and he was just humoring her like a good friend's older brother would. But no, apparently, he'd been completely oblivious.

Absolutely wild.

"You realize this is very hard for me to believe."

"I do, but it's the truth."

"Alright, so what's the moment where you finally started seeing me as a woman and not just a wee little brat?"

"It was when I came to get that soup and we went on a tour of your place."

She didn't think it was possible, but her eyes got even wider. "Wait, really? *Then!?* That seems like so long ago!"

"It's not really. I guess I'm not a very fast person, because to me, a couple of months isn't enough time for me to get over someone or fall for another. And I was in denial about my feelings for plenty of that time."

"Denial?"

"Yeah, being attracted to your little sister's lifelong friend can read as a little iffy."

"Ah, fair. I thought that crushing on my best friend's older brother was kinda violating boundaries too."

"It would have been very easy for this situation to be messy."

"But I'm glad it's not," Cici said with plenty of relief in her voice. "Even if this doesn't go anywhere, I'm happy we've at least tried."

"Yeah," Baz said softly, reaching over the table. Cici stared at his upward turned hand for a moment, something lovely blossoming in her heart. "I'm happy about that too."

Tremulously, Cici lifted her hand and slowly set it in his. He had small cracks in his palm that were stained black from his work, and thick callouses on his fingertips, and yet it was like his touch was electric against her skin. Her whole body was alight and practically vibrating, excited in a way that her panic could never touch.

It was even better than she could have possibly imagined. Sure, it was just a first date. Neither of them were declaring their love or an entire future together, and yet it was perfect nonetheless.

Because, for the first time in her life, she felt like she was finally on equal footing with Baz. Both of them on the same page, just two adults trying to do the best for themselves.

And the possibilities of it all excited her.

Conversation came and went naturally as they ate, both of them having seconds and then the baklava that Baz admitted his mother made for dessert. Even with all that, they still sat with empty plates in front of them for a couple hours until Baz's phone buzzed insistently.

Cici's heart leapt for a moment, worried that it was his ex, but she let out a sign of relief when he spoke.

"Oh, my parents want to know if it's safe to come back. When did it get to be almost eleven?"

"It's almost eleven?" Cici repeated in shock. Fishing her phone from her purse, she looked at the time and saw that indeed she'd been at his place for five full hours. "That's insane!"

"I guess time flies when you're having fun," Baz murmured. "And this has been a lot of fun. Really."

"It was fun for me too," Cici murmured. "As much as I want to be selfish, we should probably call it a night."

"Yeah, you're right. I'll tell them they can head home and then see you out."

It was a beautiful sort of melancholy that filled her as Baz texted his parents then stood, offering his hand to her once again. Cici took it, letting him walk her to the door.

But he paused on the porch, turning to her. Cici faced him as well and she could see a storm of thoughts behind his eyes.

"Penny for your thoughts?"

"I'm thinking I'm crazy for never noticing you before this year."

"That's alright. I don't know if I would have been ready before this year."

"And I'm wondering if it's too soon to kiss you."

Cici's breath hitched, and it was as if the entire world halted right then in that moment. "O-oh?"

He flushed again, taking an embarrassed step away. "Sorry, I don't want you to think I'm rushing things or that this is a rebound. I just... I haven't had this good of a night in years."

"You can kiss me," Cici blurted.

"I can?"

"Yes, please. I would like that. *A lot.*"

Cici had been kissed before, had casually dated, but she'd never had one from someone she was unequivocally in love with. She'd never really dared to think about what it would be like to really kiss Baz, but suddenly she wanted that desperately.

"Are you sure?"

She put on her firm voice, one she used oh so rarely. "Baz Gamal, if you don't kiss me right now, I might think that you're trying to be a tease."

He grinned brightly, closing the space between them again. "Well, we can't have that."

With one of his arms wrapped around her waist, he dipped his head towards hers. Gently, ever so gently, he pressed his lips against hers with the slowest of movements.

Oh *goodness.*

Cici's heels lifted from the floor as she pushed herself up into his affections, her arms winding around his shoulders. It was a tentative kiss, soft, with no sighing into each other or tongues, but it was still more than she could ever imagine.

Perfection.

She couldn't say how long they stayed like that, holding each other and sharing the first kiss of hopefully many. But when Baz did eventually pull away, she swayed slightly, her heart thundering in her chest.

"That," she had to swallow first because she was so breathless, and her throat was dry. "That was nice."

"I'm glad you approve." She swayed again but he caught her arm, pulling her to his firm chest. He smelled so good, like motor oil and pine and something else that was uniquely him. She buried her nose in his chest, just resting there. "I don't want to say goodnight."

"Me either."

Cici smiled against his chest, her smile growing that much more. "Then let's just say 'until next time'."

"Until next time, Cici."

They held each other for another moment before reluctantly parting, and Baz led her to her car. They shared one more small, chaste kiss, and then Cici drove home, feeling happier than she had in ages.

Her life was looking up. All because she'd finally found the bravery to stand up and fight for what she wanted.

Cici sang the entire way home, blasting the radio and singing off key but not caring even one bit. She was flying high and nothing could bring her down.

But apparently something could definitely send her flying higher, because when she pulled up, she saw that the porch was occupied by Papa and his lady friend. And they were *kissing*.

Cici may or may not have squealed from inside of the jeep, but she managed to contain herself into a more acceptable state as she stepped out of the vehicle. It seemed that romance was going around, which was such a wonderful, giddy thought.

Clearing her throat, she approached the porch. Like a couple of teenagers, they jumped apart and Cici swore she'd never seen Papa's face go so crimson.

"Uh, Cici, you're out late."

She was going to say something witty, perhaps even gently teasing, but all of those words left her mouth when she saw the furtive, shy way Papa looked to the librarian.

As Cici walked past her Papa on the porch, she whispered, "I'm so proud of you for being brave." Papa may have been going on in years, but his hearing was still as sharp as ever. "I know how hard that is, and it makes me so happy that you're doing something for you."

Papa didn't say anything, but he didn't have to. The librarian, wonderful woman that she was, seemed to know better than to interrupt them and stepped away to give them space.

"Thank you," Papa whispered finally, giving Cici a little squeeze. "You don't know how much it means to me for you to say that."

19

Baz

Baz felt like he was floating on cloud nine.

When Cici had first declared her intentions to court him, he'd thought she was a bit crazy. But then Victoria had shown that it was never going to work between them and he'd realized that the prospect actually wasn't that crazy at all. They got along well, they bantered like it was easier than breathing, and they shared a lot of interests. Cici was already practically a part of his family and both his sister and parents loved her.

So he'd decided he was going to call her on her courting and ask her on a date. And *wow*, had that date gone amazingly. It'd been a simple affair, just the two of them in his house, but it had been utterly perfect. He felt like he'd learned so much and he was that much closer to her.

Finally, he felt like he was on the right path.

Now it was difficult to stop himself from putting the cart before the horse and fantasizing about all the could-be's of their relationship. Especially since it was so easy. He could see himself dating her, falling in love. He could see proposing to her, merging their families together, and having their own little ones someday. He could see himself comforting her through their tribulations and her supporting him through their struggles.

It was *nice.* Really nice.

But it was also a lot, and he kept telling himself he needed to chill. After all, they hadn't even had a second date yet.

Sure, he really wanted a second date, but it had only been thirty-six hours since their first date and although he'd been out of the dating scene for plenty of time, he was pretty sure that was too soon to ask again.

But that didn't stop him from obsessively checking his phone every time he heard it buzz. Naturally, every time Sabra caught him doing it, she teased him relentlessly, and maybe he would have been annoyed if he wasn't so hyped up on everything that was happening in his life.

At least he was alone when his phone rang again and he saw it was Cici's picture on the screen. Quickly he grabbed it and answered.

"Hello?"

"Hey, Cici, what's up?"

"Oh, hey, Baz. How ya doin'?"

"You know, the usual?"

"Hiding under a car to avoid human interactions?"

"You caught me."

She let out a cute little laugh and goodness if his heart didn't skip a beat at that. It was like since he'd admitted his feelings to himself and fully let go of Victoria that his affection towards Cici had tripled. He didn't want to say that he was tipping over into infatuation, because that was unhealthy, but he sure was close.

"Hey, I know it's a bit soon, but I was wondering if maybe you'd like to do another date?"

"Another date?"

"Uh, yeah. I mean, unless it's too soon. No biggie. I just, uh..."

Baz could recognize her rising sounds of panic, so he quickly jumped in. "I'd love to."

"But you don't even know what I have planned."

"Will you be there?"

"I would certainly hope so!"

"Then I'd love to."

"Alright, fine. I was wondering if you'd want to drive two and a half hours with me to go berry picking the next state over. There's this massive farm where you can go and fill up buckets. They grow all sorts of things we can't because it's cooler there and they've got different pests."

She wanted to go berry picking with him? What an absolutely Miller thing to do.

"A two and a half hour drive, huh? Sounds like this would take most of the day."

"Yeah, we'd probably have to leave early and come back a little late if we want to stop and have dinner or something."

"You sure you won't get annoyed with me?"

"I mean, it's a risk, but it's one I'm willing to take."

That startled another laugh out of him. "Me too. It's a date."

"Yes, it definitely is. Make sure you wear something light, but long pants and sleeves. Some of those berries have some killer thorns."

"Good to know. So, this Saturday I pick you up at... let's say eight a.m?"

"Sounds like a plan. I'm looking forward to it."

Baz hung up reluctantly and may or may not have done a little victorious shuffle. His second date was in the bag with hopefully many more to come.

But first, he definitely needed to shave.

"Hey Baz, don't forget you have a fitting for your tux today!" Sabra called from the kitchen.

Okay, first he had a fitting to go to, then a shave, and then time to mentally prepare for six hours of driving and who knew how many hours of berry picking with the woman he was quickly falling in love with.

It certainly was a turn around from how his life had been going before.

And he definitely liked the change.

20

Cecilia

Cici never thought there could be so much joy in just driving down the highway with the music blasting, especially not after what happened to Cass, but if she was being honest... she was having the time of her life.

"Here comes the chorus!" Baz shouted over the rock anthem that he was blaring over the speakers.

And just like he said, the familiar notes rolled in, leaving the two of them with no other choice than to scream-sing it at the top of their lungs.

Baz had showed up exactly on time, the punctual creature that he was, and somehow Cici had managed to be ready in time, complete with baskets that Clara had woven nearly six years earlier during one of her weaving phases. While sewing, makeup and fashion were her passion, she occasionally went on what Cass called crafting sprees, which included knitting, weaving, painting, needlework and paper mâché.

She also was the one who made sure Cici was up and dressed in time, hustling her out of bed and even curling her hair into an impeccable style that looked effortless despite it taking nearly a half hour to do.

"Oh, oh, and here's the bridge!"

Cici only faltered slightly, not nearly as confident of the words as Baz was, but that didn't diminish her enjoyment at all. Her throat was gonna be sore, but she didn't mind at all.

The song ended far too soon, and she did pause it for a moment so she could take a long swig of green tea from her thermos. "We're gonna lose our voice before the day is over."

"Ehhh, you're probably right. Maybe we should take an anthem break."

"That would be the adult thing to do," Cici agreed.

"But boring."

"Oh yeah, very boring."

They exchanged a look, and then Cici turned it right back up again so they could belt it out once more. It was truly an awful cacophony of sound that would have likely had dogs howling and cats hiding in closets, but it was also incredible. Absolutely incredible.

They lasted another two classic rock songs before she dissolved into laughter and turned the music down one more time.

"Okay, now we really gotta take a rest. For real."

"Fair enough. My voice was getting a bit scratchy on that last high note."

"High note? Is that what you call that ungodly shriek you made?"

"Hey, you know the rules, no judging musical technique while on a joyride. It's illegal."

Cici snickered, settling deeper into her seat. She'd known that Baz had an impressive hotrod of a car, being a mechanic and all, but she hadn't thought the passenger's seat would be so comfortable. In fact, she'd been pretty sure it'd be the opposite.

"They must have neglected to teach me that in my driver's ed class."

Baz shook his head, clicking his tongue with mock disapproval. "The state of education these days."

"Right, because it's changed so much since your time in school, you old geezer." Playfully, she picked out one of the mints from her snack bag and pelted him with it. It was fully wrapped so she wasn't worried about it shattering or messing up his precious car, but his expression was still pretty priceless when it hit the side of his face.

"Did... did you just throw candy at me?"

"Technically it was a mint."

"Oh, a mint, of course. That changes everything."

"Exactly. Glad we're on the same page."

"You know, it's not too late to turn this car around."

"We're an hour and a half into this drive, it is absolutely too late to turn around," Cici objected with no lack of passion.

"Says who?"

"Says me, and if that's not enough, think about the environment. It'd be pretty irresponsible to use all the gas to drive this far only for us to turn around without actually achieving our goal."

"Really, you're gonna throw saving the world in on me?"

"If it gets me my way? You betcha." She sent him a wink and he leaned over to kiss her on the cheek. But to his credit, he didn't even so much as drift from his lane. That was impressive. Certainly better than Cici's own driving skills.

They swayed into discussing past people they knew and where they were currently. They used to know all the same folks, but since Baz had gone to vocational school and Cici had gone to college to get her masters, their circles had significantly widened.

Cici had had a lovely friend group in college, but they were nothing like her relationship with Sabra. Mostly because she knew that she was going to leave them behind as she moved on into a new chapter in her life. Maybe it was growing up in a small town, maybe it was from knowing she already found her platonic soulmate, but she'd always known that those she met during her college career wouldn't be permanent fixtures in her life. She cherished them nonetheless, but she didn't miss them acutely like she had Sabra while she was getting her degree.

Conversely, the employees of Baz's shop all sounded like real characters. Some of them even had ridiculous names, like Skillet. And Mr. Baxtin's story was definitely a beautiful sort of tragedy. She hoped he found happiness; he sounded like a nice guy.

Before she knew it, they were pulling off on their final exit and had only twenty minutes left of back road driving according to their GPS. She didn't think she'd ever had three hours rush by so quickly.

"Oooh, I can't wait," she said, practically bouncing in her seat. Her mouth was already almost salivating after the thought of delicious berries. While they had a fairly robust berry patch in the farthest part of the garden, there were still plenty of things they couldn't grow. Sure, they had plenty of ray berries, currants, gooseberries, elderberries and blackberries. But Papa never had much luck with strawberries, raspberries or blue berries. Ground cherries could also be hit or miss, which was a shame because those were probably Cici's favorite.

"I can't believe you brought a collapsible wagon to go berry picking. How many berries are you planning on picking?"

"Baz, they charge you by the pound here, so if you'd like to physically haul twenty or so pounds of fruit from their scale to the car, be my guest."

"You're really gonna pick that many berries?"

"That's a conversative estimate."

She could tell that Baz was looking at her out of the corner of his eye like he couldn't tell if she was being serious or not. Deciding to be a bit merciful for once, she figured a little explanation could help.

"Look, I realize for the average family of four, two to three pounds of assorted berries can go far. But even if we only count my blood relatives, there are six of us on the ranch. And if we count everyone who's actually living there, plus Savannah who can eat the same as two fully grown adults—preteen growth spurt and all that—that's actually nine mouths."

"Ah, right. I suppose I didn't."

"*And* it would be one thing if we were just gonna eat them with meals or as snacks. But you forget we're a bit of a homestead, so they'll be baked into pies or turned into cobblers. Some will be used for different lemonades and Papa might ferment some into bottles of wine to give away as gifts."

"Oh, I didn't know he made wine."

"It's a new hobby from the past couple of years he's trying out." Cici explained before continuing right on. "And then there's the preserves! Strawberry jam, blueberry jelly! Clara will also use them to make these amazing vinaigrettes to put on salads, which really helps when all the greens in the garden are starting to taste the same.

"There's cutting them up and drying them in the dehydrator for the perfect travel snack. There's Papa's patented Strawberry Rhubarb Compote, strawberry rubarb pie! Blueberry simple syrup, raspberry preserves!"

"Alright, I get it, I get it!" Baz laughed, shaking his head as he turned onto a dirt road that had to be the queue-road leading up to the entrance of the place. "I guess I had no idea that so much could be done with berries."

"Exactly! And don't get me wrong, we do a lot, a lot with everything we grow ourselves, but it's very exciting to be able to switch it up with these three that they don't grow."

"Honestly, I'm excited for you."

"You're only saying that because you think you're gonna get to taste all these delicious goodies."

"Won't I?"

Cici gave him an impish look. "Like I said, there are nine mouths in my house, so if you want some, you might have to throw down for it."

"Welp, guess I'm not getting any then."

"What, you don't think you'd win?"

"Are you kidding me? I've been familiar with Charity's biceps since we were kids. I'm pretty sure if I rolled up on any of you, she'd knock me into next Sunday." Baz paused, his brow furrowing a bit. "Actually... didn't she get in a fight with some locals at a festival a few years ago? Totally laid like three guys out?"

"Oh my gosh! I'd almost forgotten about that. It was a *great* story though." Cici chuckled to herself, remembering how Clara had spun it. It was hard to say just how much it was dramatized because it was, well, *Clara* recounting it to Cici, but it was fantastic nonetheless.

"Okay, maybe if you're *real* nice to me, I'll sneak you a treat every now and then."

"Your generosity knows no bounds."

"I know, I truly am a martyr of our time."

"Berry much so."

"Did you just..." Cici gave him an incredulous look then burst into laughter. He soon joined her, chuckling in the most pleased way. "You are *far* too young to be telling Dad jokes like that."

"Didn't you just call me an old man?"

"Hey, my wonderful quips cannot be held to any sort of continuity. They exist on their own timeline."

"Sounds complicated."

"I'm a complicated woman."

"After so many years of knowing you, yeah, I've put that together."

The car stopped and Baz put it into park, distracting Cici from whatever she was planning to say next. Surprised she looked out of the window and realized that they had parked.

Whoa, when had that happened?

She wasn't sure, but she didn't mind that time went fast with Baz. Especially if it meant that she was that close to stuffing her face with strawberries.

"Oh, we're here! Let's do this!"

"I've never seen someone so pumped for berries," Baz mused as he went to the back of the car and got her collapsible cart out of it and the buckets she'd brought. They hadn't been able to fit as many as she wanted, but that was probably for the best. Even if Cici didn't think it was possible to overbuy berries in her family.

"I guess I'm just one of a kind."

"You definitely are."

The compliment came out of nowhere, and there was a weight to his words that made Cici flush from her head all the way down to her toes. Clearing her throat, she busied herself with putting her sunhat on and sunscreen on her shoulders.

Thankfully, Baz seemed to know well enough to give her space to recover from the surprise, and they walked hand in hand to the entrance. It was surprisingly natural for their fingers to intertwine and her heart fluttered in her chest at the thought.

"So, which berry do you want to totally decimate first?"

"Let's save the strawberries for last, those are my favorite."

"Okay. I know that Sabra warned me she'd take out my knees if I didn't get her some fresh blueberries, so why don't we start there?"

"Sounds good to me!"

There were plenty of people in the world who would find picking berries both arduous and boring. There was a lot of bending, kneeling, and leaning over thick brush that some people found was too much trouble for the gain. But Cici loved it, through and through, and she was thrilled when it seemed like Baz was having almost as much fun as she was.

They laughed, they joked, they sat and took water breaks as well as talked to other people. Somehow, Cici ended up in a crowd of four children, explaining to them what berries were ripe to pick and the best way to pick them. When she finished up, she'd almost expected Baz to look impatient, but he just had the widest, cheesiest grin on his face.

"What?" she asked, more than a bit self-conscious.

"Nothing," he said without losing even an iota of his smile. "Just trying not to put the cart before the horse."

"What does that mean?" Most of the time she understood Baz, but sometimes he did manage to throw her for a loop.

"Nothing important. You think we're good on the blueberries?"

Huh. Curious. "Let's fill up this bucket and then we'll move on to raspberries."

"My mother loves raspberries," Baz said, nodding as he picked up the heavy bucket as if it didn't weight anything at all. Cici would be lying if she said she didn't take particular interest in that.

What could she say? She liked strong men and developed forearms, and Baz had both in spades.

...actually, he'd probably look pretty amazing digging with a spade, all shirtless and sweaty in the sun.

Whoa, Cici. Contain yourself, she scolded internally. It wasn't polite to ogle her date and imagine him half dressed.

Even if it was a real pretty mental picture.

Clearing her throat yet again, Cici ordered herself forward to finish out the blueberries so they could move on.

Picking raspberries was just as enjoyable as picking the blueberries had been, although it took the entire rest of the morning and into the afternoon for them to finish there. They still had eight buckets left for strawberries, and a little over four hours.

Although Cici brought plenty of snacks, her stomach certainly began to rumble around the two pm mark. She was debating whether they should give up some strawberry time to drive onto the main road and find someplace to eat, when Baz discovered that there was a food truck at the berry farm.

It turned out to have especially delicious french fries and

hamburgers, so they ended up taking a little bit longer of a break than they should have, but it left Cici feeling refueled for the biggest part of their day.

"You ready for the gauntlet?"

"Is that what we're calling it now?"

"Seems appropriate to me."

"I'd say you should reapply your sunscreen, we should refill our water thermoses, and then, we march on."

His tone dropped at the end like he was giving an inspiring speech in a military movie and Cici adored it.

"Sir yes, sir!" she said, giving a little salute before putting her sunscreen on. While she and her friends weren't always the best about sun safety, she'd long since learned that harvesting and swimming were the two activities she couldn't skimp on. Even with her trusty sunhat. She couldn't help but give Baz a little bit of a side eye, though. His skin was so beautifully, deeply golden that he rarely had to use sunscreen. It was like he just absorbed sunlight then radiated it outwards like some sort of masculine angel.

Unfair.

At least she had it better than her cousins up north. Some of them had gotten fried when they'd visited without the proper preventative measures in the middle of the summer.

When she was appropriately lathered, they headed to the strawberry fields, which according to the signs was the farthest out. Naturally. But Cici didn't mind, because Baz began to whistle a familiar melody and she hummed along, and their free hands intertwined once again.

Maybe some people dreamed of fancy balls, or luxurious vacations, but Cici's dream was stretching out all around her.

What she wanted was quality time with someone she loved, being goofy and reaping gifts from the earth.

Love. That feeling was blooming in her chest, warm and sweet, heady in it's pull. It wasn't a crushing wave like she'd heard some people say. It wasn't a whirlpool sucking her down. It was more like a comforting, contented blanket slowly tucking in around her until she was so cozy that she couldn't help but drift off into utter bliss.

If that was how she felt after just two dates with him, she couldn't wait to see what the future held.

But first, *strawberries.*

Cici's hands were red and sticky when they finally called it quits, making sure they stopped at least a half hour before close so they could weigh and load up their berries without making the employees stay late. Although Cici had been privileged enough to never have to work outside of her family ranch, she'd learned from many of her friends just how selfish and reviled it was to purposefully poke about after hours. Especially if it was a job that had a lengthy 'closing checklist'.

But, just as she hoped, they finished loading up Baz's car and pulling out of the dirt parking lot at just three minutes after six, weary, sugary and more than a bit sweaty.

And if Cici had her way, she'd do it all over again. Everything about the day was literally perfect, and she wouldn't change a single detail. From the heat of the overhead sun to the soft kiss of the car's air conditioning against her warm skin. Her mouth was prickly from the sweetness of the berries she'd eaten, which made the water in her thermos that much cooler and refreshing.

"Thank you," Baz murmured quietly, pulling her out of her blissful contemplation.

"Hmm?"

"For today. For everything. I've been so caught up in working for so long, I forgot what it was like to take time to just enjoy things."

"And you liked it?"

"I loved it."

His hand slowly slid over the middle console, palm up. It was an invitation if Cici ever saw one, just like their first date, and she placed her hand in his. Just like before, that jolt of electricity went through her, and her entire body felt so alive. So, present in the moment.

It was only then that she realized she hadn't felt a single thread of panic during the entire day. While it had been months since her last panic attack, she usually had at least a flare of alarm and worry that she had to mentally move herself through.

But nothing like that was happening today.

Only happiness, laughter and accomplishment.

It was like Baz was a balm to the storm that sometimes ravaged her emotions. A rock she could cling to. Anchor herself again. Perhaps that was far too codependent of her, but once again, her toes were curing inside of her shoes at the very idea.

She'd been daydreaming about what it would be like to date Baz for years, and who could have known it was even more amazing than she ever dared to think. Because reality didn't need dragons, or epic swordfights, or even magic to be utterly amazing.

It just needed her family, Sabra, and him.

She couldn't wait to see just how far their journey would take them. Crossing her fingers mentally, Cici hoped that it never ended.

21

———

Baz

*I*t turned out that dating Cici Miller and also going through the final details for his baby sister's wedding sure made time fly fast. Baz felt like one moment he was on the second date with Cici, and the next he was at Sabra's rehearsal dinner, patting his mother's back as she tearily recounted how her daughter had lost her first tooth to anyone who would listen.

Baz's life was so much fuller than he could have ever imagined. To think, when he'd first returned home, he'd been utterly lost. Everything that he'd tied his identity to was gone, leaving him listless and unmoored. And while his job situation still wasn't quite on stable ground, his personal life was better than ever.

He didn't feel like he was losing whole chunks of his life. He didn't feel like people were moving along without him while he was chained in the shop, always with his nose to the grind so he could make more money, so he could secure his future.

He didn't feel like he was in the rat race, permanently stuck on a wheel, constantly running to somewhere that he would never get.

Part of it was Cici, he knew that without a doubt. The way she looked at the world, the sheer joy she had just to be *alive,* made him see each day differently. It made him cherish every single moment in a way he wouldn't have before. He used to think of his time in terms of value. If he was stuck in the grocery store line too long or stuck in traffic, that was time he could have spent working and earning more money.

But lately... well, there was none of that.

It wasn't 100% Cici though. Part of it was re-falling in love with his family and the life they'd built together. Part of it was re-falling in love with the town around them. He knew his cousins up north sometimes struggled with their less loving townie neighbors, but he'd never really had that struggle where he lived. Outside of the occasional drunk or jerkwad, most people in the town wanted to just live their life and pay their bills then squeeze in some fun in between.

Baz just wished that he hadn't lost three years of his life chasing a dream in the city that would never pan out.

Granted, he'd heard that it was better to have loved and lost than to never have loved at all, and looking back, Baz could see the valuable lessons he'd learned from Victoria. From the mistakes he'd made with her and the ones she'd made with him.

And, of course, what he learned from therapy.

Because he was still going, every other week, and working on himself. He hadn't realized how much he put his self-value in his lofty ideals of 'success'. Thanks to the therapist, he was trying to dismantle that and find his self-value in healthier things that were more important to him. Like the people he loved and who loved him.

"I know that toasts are for the actual wedding, but I just want to raise my glass to all of you!" Sabra said, grinning as wide as the sun as she stood with her glass of champagne. While there wouldn't be any alcohol at the wedding, that rule wasn't in place for the rehearsal dinner, which Baz was grateful for. He was pretty sure the gentle bubbly was the only thing keeping his father from crying and even Cici looked a little teary eyed.

Okay... maybe Baz was misting up a bit too, but he was fairly sure that he was going to be able to make it until the actual wedding before shedding a tear.

"I've had the most brilliant, blessed life, and it's all thanks to every one of you. You are my family, my heart, and my soul. From my best friend who's been on uncountable adventures with me, to my big brother, who made sure we didn't run into traffic or fall out of trees...though that did happen to Cici once."

"To my parents, who came to this country with a dream and a drive and provided us with an amazing life. They picked this small town; they built the connections that allowed me to grow up in a loving community.

"I thank Mr. Ganus, my drama teacher who cast me in my first musical and I haven't looked back since. And of course, my wonderful fiancé, who has motivated me to complete my degree and be the best student who I could possibly be, and his parents, who are the best in-laws I could ever ask for.

Her voice started to crack and goodness, if Baz's heart didn't swell at that. To think, if Victoria hadn't cheated on him, he might have missed the dinner all together. Although he liked to think that he would have taken the time off, he had been such a workaholic that he couldn't be sure. After all, he'd missed three of his mother's birthdays, two of Sabras and four of his father's along with a Christmas. Not exactly a brilliant track record.

So, sitting there and watching his sister's eyes brim with tears, hearing the love she had pouring out across the table, Baz knew he never wanted to miss another moment. It just wasn't worth it.

"So cheers to all of you! Here's to tomorrow and all the memories we'll make from here until forever!"

"From here until forever!" Everyone echoed. But when Baz repeated his sister's words, his gaze couldn't help but linger on Cici. With her pink lips pressed ever so delicately to her glass, her long hair flowing over one shoulder, her intense gaze full of love and adoration...

He had to admit, forever would be *real* nice.

THEY WERE PLAYING HERE COMES the bride.

Baz had one last moment to compose himself before he watched his sister get walked down the aisle. He took a deep breath, steeled himself for the onslaught of emotions, then gazed towards the doors that he knew his sister would be coming through.

There was a *very* pregnant pause, and then finally the attendants pulled them open, revealing Sabra in all her glory, and their very much crying father.

She looked *beautiful*. Truly gorgeous and radiating like the sun. Baz couldn't help but think back to when he'd first been introduced to her. She had been a red faced, crying baby and he'd been just over three years old. He vaguely remembered being unimpressed and wanting to go home to his juice box.

He guessed he was hard to impress as a child.

But he also remembered when everything changed on that. She'd been learning to crawl, able to make happy sounds and concerned noises, when she'd fallen. Baz had been in the living room, watching his favorite cartoon, when he'd heard her pained shriek. In an instant, his entire world changed, and suddenly he knew he needed to protect the little crying creature that was his sister from anything that might hurt her.

And now he was handing that responsibility off to another man.

Sure, he would always be her big brother, nothing would ever change that, but they weren't going to live together. She was going to be building a new life with her own house and children and so many new memories. He couldn't be happier.

And when he looked to Cici in her beautiful bridesmaid dress, he saw a future where he could possibly have that happiness too.

The soft, gossamer blue of her dress made her eyes pop that much more, even if they were rimmed slightly red with unshed tears. The smile on her face was so genuine, her love for Sabra clearly overflowing.

Baz felt much the same.

The music swelled as she approached her groom, and all too soon, they were kissing. Once more Baz felt like if he blinked, the entire world might pass him by. Suddenly she was no longer Sabra Bashyrah Gamal, but rather Sabra Bashyrah Quinn.

Sister. Daughter. Wife. And all-around wonderful person.

Baz had finally reached his limit, and as the two ran out with people throwing flower petals over their heads, his first tear escaped. He wasn't sobbing, like his mother, but he couldn't pretend he was unmoved.

But that's okay, because he didn't want to be unmoved. He wished it was possible to record exactly what he was feeling so he could revisit it again and again and again. His heart was so full, but at the same time he felt like he had room for so much more.

Thankfully, photos didn't take forever. Baz had been to a couple of weddings where they made their guests wait a couple of hours before the reception because they wanted to do a very involved photoshoot, and he hated it every time. It wasn't his wedding, so he hadn't had an absolute say in what happened, but he'd strongly encouraged Sabra to at least have appetizers out for those attending and to have a simple shoot close by.

Thankfully, she listened, and after less than forty-five minutes, the women were going off to change into their reception dresses before joining everyone else in the reception hall.

He knew back when Sabra was planning to fund everything herself, they'd had a tiny little church venue picked out. But thanks to the Millers, they'd rented out a lovely sort of farm place about a half hour outside of town that had a beautiful pond and a man-made babbling brook over a meticulously placed stone and a massive pavilion. It was perfect, but of course it was, because the Millers were pretty amazing with their resources.

Actually, the Millers were just pretty amazing in general. Especially Cici.

Baz kept looking towards the reception door, waiting for her to appear. If he was being objective, Sabra and her three bridesmaids actually got changed quite quickly, and soon they joining the rest of the reception and it was time to officially begin the festivities.

There were speeches, there was a slideshow, there were tears and there were toasts. It was wonderful, in every sense of the word. But there was still something Baz was anxious for.

And that was a dance.

A dance with none other than Cici Miller, the woman he'd been dating for just about a month. They'd done a lot of things together since that first date at his house. Dinner at each other's houses, plenty of picnics, berry picking, swimming and even ridiculously close seats at a monster truck rally the next city over.

But they hadn't danced together yet. And although Cici had definitely come way more down to earth than she was when she was younger, Baz still wanted to give her that fantasy. While he wasn't into the same fantasy genres that she loved, he knew enough that the hero/heroine always got that perfect romance at the end of the book.

But the father-daughter dance was first, and then the bride and groom dance. Naturally Baz didn't want either of those to rush by. He cherished them, storing them into his mind as fond memories that he would be able to recall for the rest of his life. But there was a simmering sort of eagerness just under the surface of his skin.

Finally, it was the first dance to the full wedding and he made a beeline right for Cici. He didn't care if he looked overeager. He didn't care if most of the bridal party was rushing to the food tables to get their plates.

Of course, she saw him and the way her whole face lit up made his heart skip a beat. Even after three years with Victoria she never looked at him like *that*.

But if he was being fair, he didn't think he'd ever looked at her like that either. He had been so busy preparing for the future that he'd neglected the Victoria of the present. While it wasn't his fault she cheated on him, it was his fault for forgetting to actually *enjoy* their relationship until she felt so lonely that she was practically single.

He'd learned from that, though, and he was never going to make that same mistake again.

"Hey Baz. You look dashing today. Special occasion?"

"You could say that," he said, knowing he was grinning like a loon and not caring one bit.

"What a coincidence, I happened to be dressed for a special occasion too."

"And don't you look amazing for it. Whoever you're going with must be a very lucky man."

"Yes, yes he is."

She gave him that impish grin of hers that never failed to make his blood rush through his veins. She really was something.

"Miss Cecilia Miller, would you do me the honor of this dance?"

And there it went, the impish grin faded into a much sweeter one, with a primrose pink flush of color across those high cheekbones of hers.

"Why, I thought you'd never ask."

She lifted her hand and Baz took it, hearing a not very well contained squeal from Clara, who was just a table away. But even that sound couldn't distract him from Cici, his eyes locked onto her and only her as they practically floated to the dance floor.

Baz would never claim to be particularly coordinated or graceful, but the day after he'd gotten back from berry picking, he'd asked Sabra to help him work out at least a few moves. She'd said it was gross to dance with her own brother, so she recruited one of her friends named Gem.

Wait... that wasn't right. Ginny? Genivieve? No... Gemini! Right, she'd been flirty at first but once Sabra had casually mentioned that Baz and Cici were dating, the woman had cooled it and was an amazing teacher. They practiced together every day, and he was now somewhat comfortable with a slow dance and slightly faster ones. He was definitely going to have to send the girl a thank you gift.

But Gemini would have to wait for another day, because at the moment, he only had eyes for Cici.

"I haven't danced with somebody since the eighth grade," she murmured, cheeks a beautiful, blushing pink.

"I find that hard to believe," Baz murmured. He knew that his voice was impossibly low, but he was afraid that if he spoke too loudly that the entire scene would disappear like a dream. He didn't know it was possible to fall in love so hard, so fast, but that was exactly the situation that he was in. It was like one of Cici's or Sabra's fantasy books, one where soulmates and true love existed. He felt pulled to her, and seen in a way that he never had with anyone else before.

"Well, I suppose Sabra and I did go with each other to prom, but that doesn't count."

"Maybe I'm selfish, but part of me is very pleased that I'm your first real dance of your adult life."

"That's alright, you're allowed to be impressed. I just hope that you're just as impressed the hundredth time we dance."

Baz didn't think it was possible, but his heart filled again, growing larger and larger as it tried to cram in all the love he felt for the incredible woman in his arms. "That's a lot of weddings to go to."

"Who said we could only dance at weddings?" Cici said, her voice just as low as Baz's. Her face was tilted up towards him, lips and cheeks so pink, eyes scanning his face like they were searching for something. Whatever she was looking for, Baz wanted to give it to her. "We don't need an event to dance."

"No, I suppose we don't, do we?"

The slow song they were dancing to faded into another, the melody wrapping around them like an encore, urging them to stay in the moment. And Baz was just fine with that. If he had his way, they would stay there in their demi-waltz forever, just them, the music, and whatever was growing between them.

It was like they were in perfect sync, moving to the lilt together, never stepping on each other's toes. Baz didn't think he'd ever been so coordinated in his entire life. But he was grateful for the blessing. Grateful for the way Cici was looking up at him, a nobody. Grateful to have her in his arms.

All of the emotions flooded him, overwhelming and wonderful, so he did the only thing he could do; dip his head down and capture her lips in his.

It wasn't a demanding kiss, not in a public place in front of all their relatives. But it was sweet, full of emotion, longing, and all the happiness that Baz felt. He hoped that Cici could feel just how important she was to him through it. He hoped that she could feel his gratitude in it, and his promise to always try to be the best he could be for her.

And Cici, the saint that she was, kissed him back. There wasn't a hint of hesitance or worry to her. No, she kissed him back and sighed into it, melting against his body as they continued to move across the floor.

Baz could have just held her like that forever, dancing and kissing and lost in their own little worlds. But eventually, the song changed again, and someone cleared their throat from beside them.

"I'd hate to interrupt, but I'd like to have this dance, if that's alright."

Baz looked to the giant of a man beside them, standing with his hand outstretched. He looked only vaguely familiar, but Cici smiled broadly at him.

"Bart! It's so good to see you! Where's Missy?"

"She's taking a break with the baby, so I figured I might as well come over and steal a dance with my baby cousin."

Cici looked to Baz, a blush to her cheeks. "You don't mind, do you?"

"Of course not." Although Baz could have danced with her forever, he knew better than to come between Cici and her family. Besides, he lived in the same town as her. It wouldn't be very kind to hog her over her cousin she only got to see once or twice a year. "I'll go get us a couple of plates. See you at the table?"

"That sounds perfect."

With a gentlemanly nod to Bart, who really was a hulk of a man, Baz headed to do just that. But he didn't quite make it there before Sabra intercepted him.

"How about a brother-sister dance?"

He narrowed his eyes, looking around her as if expecting some sort of trap. "I thought you said that sibling dancing was gross."

"Yeah, when you're asking your sibling to learn how to dance romantically with the woman you're dating. But this is different. It's just for us, the Gamal kids."

Now that, Baz couldn't argue with. "That I can do."

The dance was different than the one with Cici. For one, it was a faster paced song, and for second, they were much sillier together with some tickling, some poking and plenty of teasing thrown around. But it was exactly what Baz wanted.

It also reassured him. There was a small voice inside of him that whispered Sabra was going to leave him behind. That her life was going to change forever and there would be no room in it for him. But even married, Sabra was still Sabra. She was going to do what she wanted, love as fiercely as she could, and never abandon those she cared about.

He really was the luckiest man in the world. Whether his parents, his sister, or his girlfriend, he knew he was surrounded by good people. Not a lot of folks could say that.

Then, after his sister, his mother wanted a dance and of course he wasn't going to say no to her! He never quite did get back to the table to get food, because after that, Cici snatched him up for one of those cheesy line dancing things that seemed to be so popular at American weddings.

When they finally did get a rest, his feet were hurting, and he was more than prepared for the delicious spread the Millers had ordered from their favorite caterer. Baz remembered being half surprised that Clara wasn't cooking the whole thing herself, but apparently she did have a few limits.

"Oh my gosh, if I don't get food in me right now, I might start eating the flower arrangements." Cici said, squeezing his hand as she slowly walked to the bridal party table. She'd confessed to him before that she wasn't very good at walking or moving in high heels, so he guessed her feet were hurting her. If she let him, he'd give her a nice, long foot rub later.

Heck, he'd rub her feet every single night until the day he died if it meant she would stay in his life.

"How about you sit down and I go fill a plate for you? That way your feet get to rest?"

She looked at him like he had offered to lay down his life for her, not get her food. "Would you?"

"Yeah, I'd be happy to."

"Bless your heart. Extra strawberry rhubarb pie for you, next week."

"You don't have to bribe me, but also, consider that bribe taken." He didn't know how he'd gone twenty-seven years in his life without tasting Papa Miller's incredible confection, but it had become one of his top three desserts in just a single bite.

Cici laughed, holding his hand right up until he deposited her into her chair, then he was off to fill their plates. Thankfully, there was still plenty of food despite the quite large crowd.

Back when it had been the Gamals taking care of things, they'd been uncertain if they could afford even twenty guests. Which was quite awkward considering that Philip, the groom, had four siblings and seven aunts who were all married.

But again, the Millers had come and saved the day so that all of Philip's siblings could come as well as their plus ones and children, as well as his aunts and uncles in laws, *and* a multitude of the Millers themselves.

Naturally not every single one of the three clans could come, that was basically a hundred people on it's own. But Charity, Alejandro and Savannah were there along with Cass and her beau, Charlie and his girl, and Clara. Apparently, Clara did have a lovely gentleman that she was courting, but he was recovering from a new skin graft and couldn't be around so many people without risking his life.

He admired Clara that she just showed up anyways, happy to be there for her sister's best friend. She had a good heart, that one. It was easy to see how Cici survived her rather traumatic childhood with kind people in her life like that.

Plates now thoroughly loaded with food, Baz hurried back to the table and set it in front of Cici with his usual flourish. Her eyes went wide and her hands went over her heart, the most adorable gasp escaping her lips.

"Did I mention I love you?" she cooed, already reaching for her fork.

"Uh... no, actually."

They both froze, realization creeping across Cici's face in horrified little ticks.

"Did... did I just drop the 'l' bomb over food?"

"You most certainly did."

She looked up at him finally, cheeks a flaming red but a touching sort of earnestness in her eyes. "I'm sorry. Not the most romantic way for this to happen but, uh, I guess it's true. And kind of scary."

"I understand," he answered, bending forward so he could press his lips to hers once more, the food between them forgotten. "Because I love you too. And I know it's too fast, and probably too soon after Victoria, but I can't help how I feel. I love you. Cecilia Miller. I love you so much that it hurts, and I never want it to stop hurting."

Tears were in her eyes again, and this time it was her who started the kiss. And the next one. And the one after that. When they finally stopped, she threw her arms around his shoulders despite the awkward angle they were at.

"I'm glad we're on the same page."

"Me too," Baz admitted. "And I want on the same page with you, no matter where our book goes."

There was another gentle throat clearing beside them and Baz finally straightened, realizing there was an older woman standing next to him.

"Oh, hello there, Mrs. Vangella," Cici said, because of course she recognized everyone. "It's so good to see you."

"It's good to see you as well! I didn't know you were dating someone! You certainly do keep it on the downlow."

"Ah, you know how it is, I don't get off the ranch much."

Baz just smiled absently. He didn't know who the woman was but clearly Cici liked her, so he would be friendly and polite.

"I understand! I remember being young and busy, long ago." She let out a good-natured, old lady laugh. "So, when are the two of you tying the knot? I saw your dance out there! You're practically prepared for the wedding already!"

If Cici was red before, she turned utterly crimson, even her ears shining brightly with blood. She stammered a few things, clearly taken off guard, but then it was Baz who was clearing her throat.

"That depends on her, mostly. I've already got the perfect ring in mind and I'm just waiting for the right time."

There was another gasp from Cici, this one even louder than the last. It was a risk admitting what he'd done, but after their confession to each other, how could he not be as honest as possible with her?

"Really?" she said, voice at a much higher octave than normal, looking so absolutely adorable.

"Goodness," the old lady said, fanning herself. "Did I accidentally unlock a secret!"

"Really," Baz said, turning to Cici completely. "I know where my happiness lies, and I'll wait however long you need to get there too. I just pray that you will."

"I... I don't know what to say!"

"You don't have to say anything, but I wouldn't say no to another kiss!"

"I think I can give you one of those."

And so he picked her up off her feet kissed her. Then set her gently back down on the ground so she could throw her arms around him yet again and kiss him with all she had.

"Well then," the forgotten woman said next to them. "I'll leave you lovebirds to it! Congratulations!"

Normally Baz would break away to at least say goodbye, but it wasn't every day he got to experience a kiss from someone who he just practically told he wants to marry.

When they did break apart, they were both panting and Cici's lipstick was smeared below her lip. Lovingly, Baz wiped it away with her thumb, and she leaned into his hand.

"Should we dance again?" she murmured, staring up at him like he was the entire world.

"I thought you were hungry."

"I can eat later. Right now, I only want to be close to you."

"Then yeah, let's dance."

Laughing, he pulled her onto the dance floor where they joined their families. It felt like a new chapter was opening up in their story, and Baz was thrilled to see how it went.

He wasn't kidding about that ring, though.

EPILOGUE: BAZ

Six months had passed since his little sister's wedding and time made absolutely zero effort to slow down.

About two weeks after Sabra came back from her honeymoon, Baz returned to work. It was tempting not to, but his savings account *was* getting low and he didn't want to just mooch off his parent's spare room forever.

However, with so much at home to look forward to, he quickly came to resent the long commute to the city. It stole time from him every day, time that could be spent with his family or with Cici.

With his hour and twenty minutes spent in his car, Baz began to start daydreaming about opening a shop in town. Mr. Baxtin even offered to buy him out of his third of the shop since it was flourishing, so Baz could be freed up to use the money as a way to start his own business.

But unfortunately, his credit wasn't good enough to get everything he would need. It'd be expensive to open up a shop.

Bank after bank refused him and there wasn't anything he could do about that, so he resolved to just save as much as he could and try again in three years.

But he wasn't going to lose himself to the grindstone again. He was all about balance. Balance and enjoying all the blessings in his life.

Because he sure had a lot of them.

...even if the last month had been a little rocky.

Cici had told him from the beginning of them dating that sometimes she would get massively busy with ranch stuff and it would seem like she disappeared, but really she was just doing the harvest or spring crunch. But even though she'd told him, he wasn't quite prepared for just how much she would be occupied.

Suddenly their hang out time went from seeing each other three times a week to barely even once. It seemed every time he contacted her, she had a different excuse. From planning Charity's wedding to helping Daisy connect with some animal-rescuing cousin Cici had up north to save a herd of horses, to needing to help Papa with his seedlings.

Even though she warned him, even though he knew better, his mind couldn't help but keep going back to his ex when her behavior had suddenly become dodgy and erratic. He did try to push those thoughts down every time they cropped up, but that was easier said than done.

So, he tried to be patient, going to work and living for the weekend when he could see Cici more reliably. It wasn't a guarantee, but he'd long since learned he was much more likely to see her on a Saturday or Sunday.

Naturally, when he woke up to a text from her, he happily opened it with excitement already sparking through him.

Come downstairs when you're ready.

Come downstairs? Baz blinked at the message for a long moment before it clicked, and then he was tossing himself out of bed.

He didn't think he'd ever brushed his hair, washed his face, brushed his teeth then gotten dressed so quickly. But he certainly had plenty of motivation considering just how rare any time with Cici was lately.

Thundering down the stairs, he saw her sitting at the table, looking exquisite in a pastel sundress and her hair pulled back into a high ponytail. She'd started wearing it that way lately, and it looked really good on her.

"Hey there, handsome."

"Good morning, beautiful," he said, bounding over to her and placing a kiss on her cheek. She tilted her face towards him, letting him plant a few pecks, before gesturing to the table.

"Believe it or not, I made all this."

"Incredible. What's the occasion?"

"Just missing you and your family. Figured it would be nice to start our day together."

"Oh, did Sleeping Beauty finally wake up?" his father said, coming in from the garage with a fresh bag of coffee beans. "I'll get this started then and fetch your mother."

Cici blushed slightly when Baz raised an eyebrow at her. "I don't know how to use your coffee machine..." she admitted.

"That's alright. I think I remember your family uses a percolator and a French press?"

"Um, I think Charlie does. We're mostly a tea family because of Papa and Clara."

"Right, I knew that."

"Sure you did." She sent him a wink then sat down, and he seated himself right next to her. There was a strange energy to the air, but he couldn't quite put his finger on it. It felt like every time he quickly glanced to his parents that they were smiling. Like they knew something he didn't. Strange.

But even with that feeling, the meal was fantastic. Cici caught him up on some of the highlights of the horse rescue as well as Savannah's performance at the school talent show. Baz really loved how much the Miller family had basically adopted the preteen even before Charity's wedding and his mind would always wander to what it would be like for a new baby in that family.

Granted, thinking of new babies made him think of *Cici* having a baby, and what it would be like to be a father. He wasn't in a rush, but he wouldn't be very honest if he tried to deny that he always wanted a family. Three or four little ones to love and cherish and also probably spoil at least a little bit.

"Why are you staring at my stomach?" Cici asked curiously, looking down her front. "Do I have a stain?"

"Huh?" Oh no, he'd really been staring, hadn't he? Poor move on his part. "No, just admiring the pattern."

"Uh-huh…"

She narrowed her eyes at him but thankfully let it go, and they finished up the meal with more fun stories and laughter. But as they were sitting there in front of their empty plates, an unreasonably loud honk sounded from outside.

"Who the heck is that?" Baz grumbled. "It's way too early on the weekend to be making that much noise."

Cici shrugged and then the horn sounded again. "If it's bothering you, you could go ask them to stop."

"It's not bothering you?"

Another shrug. Huh, strange. Cici very rarely didn't have an opinion on things. "Eh."

It honked again.

"I'm gonna see if I can put a stop to this."

Standing up, Baz strode to the door and threw it open, ready to confront whoever was making a racket.

Just about the last thing he expected to see was Charlie's RV in front of his house.

"Hey there, Mr!" the only Miller brother called from the driver's seat, half hanging out the window. "Your chariot awaits!"

"My what?"

And out of nowhere, Sabra's upper half popped out of another window on the side. "Yeah, ya slowpoke! Get in!"

"What is going on?" he asked, looking over his shoulder to see Cici and his parents calmly getting to their feet and crossing to him. But his girlfriend just had an enigmatic look on her face as she squeezed by him.

"You heard them. Better not keep your chariot waiting. It'd be so sad if it turned into a pumpkin."

Baz sputtered for a moment, but then his parents moved past him too until he was the only one in the room.

"Well, when in Rome, I suppose..."

Grabbing his own keys, he locked the door and hurried into the RV.

He was bewildered, that was for sure, but every time he asked a question, people either blatantly ignored him or changed the subject. It probably would have been more frustrating if he wasn't in the massive, high tech RV, surrounded by the people he loved.

"Are you going to tell me what's going on?" Baz asked for probably the dozenth time in five minutes, leaning in close to Cici.

"We're taking a ride in my brother's RV."

"Yeah, but *why?*"

"Do we need a reason."

"Um, generally, yes."

"Hmm, I disagree."

Baz knew he wasn't going to get anywhere with her, not when she looked so pleased with herself, so he contented himself with looking out the window.

It looked like they were driving to the opposite side of town. Not that it was that far, but it had certainly grown by quite a bit since he left for the city. It was only maybe a quarter mile more of main street and maybe four or so streets connected to it, but it looked like there was another extension being added on.

Who knew, maybe in twenty years or so, their quaintly small town would be more like an incredibly small city.

Baz wasn't sure if he liked that idea or not.

He was quickly distracted from that quandary, however, when the RV slowed to a stop.

"Huh, is this all new construction?" he asked, spotting several new houses and several works in progress. At least they all appeared to be fairly different in structure. Baz hated the subdevelopments he saw in the city and wealthy suburbs where all the places looked exactly the same, like someone had carbon copied them and just rotated them slightly for variation.

"Let's go check it out and see," Cici said, grabbing his hand.

She led him out of the RV but he noticed that it was in a very particular way, so that once they were outside, his view was largely blocked by the RV. Everyone else piled out as well, lining up around him like it was for a photo or something.

"Whatever you have planned, I hope you get to it soon, because this is getting weird."

"Just be patient," Cici assured, squeezing his hand before yelling to her brother. "Ready, Charlie?"

"Ready!"

"Alright, pull away!"

The RV hardly made any noise, fancy thing that it was, and then it was pulling away, revealing what was undeniably a mechanic's shop that was almost near completion. It was brand new and shining, almost like it was polished.

"What is this..." Baz trailed off when his eyes landed on the practically sparkling sign, which had what looked like a professional version of the doodle he'd sketched in one of his notebooks. He'd started doing that after his therapist had encouraged him to plan and dream ahead, but put it down in a physical space so he would have a concrete thing to look at instead of getting lost in the abstract. He hadn't been aware that anyone had ever noticed him writing or drawing in them.

Then again, Cici doodled all the time. She'd even given him some of those doodles in her courting basket.

"Cici," he whispered, hardly daring to breathe. "What is this?"

"What does it look like?" Cici asked, that mischievous grin spreading across her beautiful features.

"It looks like a mechanic's shop with my logo on it."

"Well that makes sense, because that's exactly what it is."

Baz stared. Baz blinked. Baz sputtered and looked from her to the shop and back.

"Happy birthday!" Everyone cried, even Charlie from the RV parked just a bit away.

Baz couldn't give an exact estimate to how long he stood there, completely offline, but when he did speak, he didn't know where to start.

"It's not my birthday for another two and a half weeks."

"I know," Cici said, leaning against him and pressing a kiss to his cheek. "But I figured you would want your opening day on your actual birthday."

"Opening day?" Baz echoed.

She was giving him a shop?

Was he in the real world or just in a particularly convincing dream?

"Is this really happening?"

"It is, don't worry! And if two and a half weeks isn't enough to do the finishing touches and have your opening day, you can have it whenever you want. I just wanted to give you options."

"Options, right."

"And this is one hundred percent yours, you're the sole owner. We do have to get to the bank so I can transfer all the accounts I used to set this up over to you, but other than that, it's yours and yours alone."

Baz couldn't help but gawk at Cici. She was happy, that much was obvious, but how could she be so casual about handing over his dream to him?

"You did this for me?"

That look crossed her face, the one when she was feeling especially syrupy and romantic. "Of course, Baz. I believe in you. I believe in your business. I believe in your dream and I believe in *us*. Your parents helped a little too of course. And Papa was more than happy to assist."

A shyer smile crossed her features. "Besides, I'm being a little selfish."

"How on Earth could anything about this be selfish?"

"It's a pain that you have to drive so far away for work. I figure if you have a job in town, you'll spend less time commuting and more time with me. Plus, I can visit you for lunches."

"If this is you being selfish, I can't wait to see what being generous is."

"Keep up the good behavior, and you just might fight out."

"Promises, promises," was all that Baz managed before he needed to sweep her up and kiss her silly. Applause sounded from all of his family and hers around him, a cacophony of support. He felt like he was going to burst, he was so excited.

Just nine months earlier, his entire world had fallen apart and he'd been more lost than he'd ever been in his life. But with Cici by his side, everything had turned itself around. He had a healthy relationship, better habits with his work/life balance, he got to see his family more and he no longer felt like his dreams were permanently outside of his reach.

And now he *had his own shop!!!*

Picking Cici up, he swung her around, kissed her some more, hugged her some more and laughed until he felt like he was going to cry.

"Alright, alright, set me down before I get dizzy and ruin the moment!" Cici cried, giving his forehead a peck. Baz complied, but she was in for all the shoulder and foot rubs she wanted for a solid week a least. He was going to pamper her so much she was going to be sick of him when all was said and done.

"Well, are you ready for the tour inside? Mr. Baxtin and the guys at your other shop made sure I ordered all the right things you'd need, and they even helped haul a lot of your stuff over here last night."

"What? Really? You've got to be kidding me."

"Nah, you've got an amazing crew there. And even though

you won't be working with them much anymore, you should still keep in touch with them. As friends, ya know."

"Yeah, that's not a bad idea."

Baz looked over the small shop and the four-car garage attached to it. It was the perfect size for their small town. It was just perfect in general.

"So, about that tour?"

Looking down, he realized that Cici had extended her hand and was looking at him expectantly.

"Yeah, of course. Lead the way!"

She did, and his family followed after them, all of them going into their new future together.

And what a future it was.

EPILOGUE: CECILIA

"Do you want to hear this terrible pun I read today?"

Cici looked up from her phone, her mouth full of roast. She tried not to have her phone out during meals, but with Clara and Nathan on vacation, it was the only way she could keep in touch with her middle sister, and they'd been in the middle of a lengthy text-chain when the roast had finished.

"Lay it on me," she said once she swallowed.

In the year and a half since they'd started dating, they'd both told some terrible puns to each other. Cici blamed Clara, who had a borderline obsession with bad jokes.

"Why was the computer late for work?"

Cici took another bite of her meal, chewing it over as she also chewed over the pun.

"Ummm, something about a terabyte?"

"Because he had a *hard drive.*"

"Oh *boooooo,* that's terrible."

"Your groan only makes me more powerful."

"You need to stop hanging out with my sister. She's a terrible influence on you."

"I think you mean *amazing* influence on me. I've never been so armed with goofy jokes."

Cici couldn't help but laugh, and in that long moment of laughter, everything hit her so acutely. It was like eighteen months of emotions and ideas all swamped her, and she was swept up in the rush of it.

So much had happened. Charity's wedding. Cass's wedding. Nathan needing a kidney transplant. Clara's engagement. Savannah becoming an actual teenager. Papa and his lady friend getting engaged. Charity and Alejandro announcing that they were looking to adopt.

And Baz was with her through it all. He'd laughed with her, he'd cried with her, he'd held her hand when she'd had a panic attack as well as when they went on walks around the ranch together.

His face was lined with beautiful memories, and his hands were lined with the future she wanted to spend with him.

She almost couldn't breathe, she was so struck by everything she felt for the man standing in front of her. Who knew that it would be a terrible pun who triggered that switch in her, but suddenly, Cici knew without a doubt that Baz was the only one for her.

"I'm ready," she managed to croak eventually.

"Pardon?" Baz gave her a confused look, because how could he not be confused? One moment they were joking around, the next Cici was having an existential revelation.

"I'm ready," she repeated, feeling her strength return to her.

She was able to repeat it a little more firmly, and sat up straighter.

"Uhhh, did I forget something? Were we going out today? You're ready for what?"

"For you to ask me to marry you."

She'd never forgotten his confession from Sabra's wedding. That he was already so sure about them that he'd picked out a ring. Part of her had been tempted to say yes right then and there, but she knew better. And... technically he hadn't asked her to marry him, just stated that he had picked out a ring.

Cici loved him, Cici had wanted to marry him eventually, but thankfully she'd had the clarity of mind to know that she wasn't ready. She was an adult, sure, but only barely an adult, and still largely figuring out what that meant. She'd only just graduated from college and was figuring out what it was like to be back on the ranch full time as well as be the master of her own destiny.

But she'd been home a little over two years and she felt more comfortable in her skin than she had ever been. She knew who she was, and aside from the growth that naturally came from getting older and wiser, she knew what she wanted and what she was about.

So yeah, she was ready to marry Baz. She was ready to dedicate their futures to each other and she knew she was ready to make that promise.

...but maybe she shouldn't have blurted it over breakfast after a pun about computers.

Oh no, Baz was staring at her. He wasn't saying anything and he was staring at her. It was a much rarer occasion that her panic spiked up, but it certainly was in the silence of the room.

She'd ruined it. She hadn't meant to, but somehow she'd

turned what should have been an incredibly romantic moment into an awkward one.

"Alright," he said finally. "I just need some time."

He needed time? Was he regretting saying that all those months earlier? Had he been lying about the ring? No, none of that seemed like Baz. He was a romantic, sure, and he always meant what he said.

"...what do you need time for?" she whispered fearfully. It seemed even with all her work on herself, sometimes a strong surprise could knock her off balance and send those little tendrils of doubt and anxiety creeping up into her brain.

But the grin Baz sent her was both soft and sweet. "Didn't you once spend a month secretly buying and setting up a shop for me so you could do a grand reveal two weeks before my birthday?"

Cici flushed at that. It was one of her most amazing memories and she was particularly proud of it. Baz had lit up like a kid at Christmas and she'd definitely logged it under one of the best days ever. Although it had been a present for Baz, it had still ended up being a magical time for Cici too.

Immediately, she calmed, because how could she deny her boyfriend that giddy feeling of pulling off something particularly special for someone he loved. Taking a deep breath, she gave him a nod.

"Just so you know, it was actually six months of work. I started on it after the wedding when you mentioned you didn't want to go back to work in the city because it made you feel like you were losing so much time."

At that Baz's eyes went wide. "Six months?"

"Six months."

He shook his head, chuckling at her in the pleasant, rumbling way of his. "You're incredible, you know that."

Cici didn't hold anything back when she answered. "You make me feel that way, yeah."

It wasn't often that she could make Baz blush, but she loved it every time she did. His cheeks flushed in front of her, physical proof of how much she could affect him.

"...I promise I won't make you wait six months for my big reveal, but you're not gonna know when it's coming."

"Well, when you say it like that, it's almost ominous."

"Oh no, nothing ominous. I just promise to give you a memory our grandchildren will brag about."

"Grandchildren? I think we're skipping a step there."

"Maybe," Baz said, chuckling. "But we've got all the time we need to figure it out."

Cici loved the fall festival.

She'd managed to come back to it twice during college, but she'd missed four of them as well, one of those including the one where her siblings got into a brawl. Cici couldn't believe her luck and had sworn to herself that she'd never miss another one as long as she could help it.

"I am so hungry," Savannah said, patting her stomach. The girl had shot up so she was nearly as tall as Charity, and she still ate about as much as one would expect an explosively growing teenager to eat. "I love festival food!"

"Trust me," Cici said, her hand in Savannah's. "We're gonna eat ourselves silly."

"I'm going to hold you to that!"

Cici nodded as they walked along. Normally their family tried to go as a unit, but between Papa and Charity running his stall, Cass wanting to sleep in for a bit, Baz having his two employees call in, and Charlie and Daisy doing pony rides for the children, they all had different times where they would actually be free. But Cici didn't mind. She figured she could do an early afternoon circuit where she stuffed herself, napped behind Papa's stall, and then walk around with whoever was free for a couple games and rides as night fell.

It was going to be a grand fall festival; she was sure of it. But what she didn't expect was for Sabra and her fiancé to practically jump out in front of her when she passed through the pretty, vibrant banners marking the entrance.

"Uh... hey guys. Something up?"

Cici wasn't sure if a million years could have prepared her for what happened next. Abruptly, Savannah pulled her hand away and cheerful music started to play from... actually, she didn't know where.

"Do you guys hear that?"

They definitely did, because the next thing Cici knew, they were beginning to dance. Why were they dancing? Had she passed out in the fall heat and hit her head?

She didn't know, but her feeling of incredulousness didn't fade as Sabra placed a sash over her head and she was herded to the right, where a lot of the vendor stalls were usually arranged.

And the vendor stalls were all there, but their owners weren't in them. Instead, they were all standing in a line, waving scarves, banners and even flags, lip syncing the words of the peppy music. Cici barely had time to look down the long row before more townsfolk rushed in and began to twirl, dancing to the lyrics that Cici was only just beginning to comprehend.

Is it that look in your eyes? Or just this dancing juice?
Hey baby, I think I want to marry you!

"Oh my gosh," Cici breathed, shock jolting through her that she stopped right then and there. But Savanna's arm wrapped around her, urging her onward again. Where, almost impossibly, a small but beautiful, simple carriage was pulled out from between two tents by one of her family's horses. "This can't be real. This can't!"

Don't say no, no, no, no, no!
Just say yeah, yeah, yeah, yeah, yeah!
And we'll go, go, go, go, go,
If you're ready, like I'm ready!

It was a work of art, made out of polished wood and absolutely covered in flowers. Cici could recognize Charity's handiwork anywhere, and her heart lurched in her chest.

They knew. They all knew, and they all planned this just for *her*.

Tears rushed in. She was laughing, she was crying, and it was just so perfect. The music was swelling around her, and if there was ever magic in the real world, this was it.

Another hand slipped into hers and she looked over to realized Papa was standing next to her, tears in his eyes too.

"Come on, baby girl. It's time."

Nodding, she let him lead her to the carriage, hand in hand. The whole town was cheering, singing and dancing for her. It was better than any movie or book she'd ever read, because it was real. And it was *hers*!

Carefully, she stepped up into the carriage and settled in the cushiony seat. After another line of music, Charlie emerged from behind one of the tents, dressed up like an old-fashioned carriage driver, complete with a top hat. With a simple wink, he got onto the horse and gave it a soft order to trot along.

Cause it's a beautiful night,
We're looking for something fun to do.
Hey baby, I think I wanna marry you!

It was a dream, a perfect, *perfect* dream. Still stunned, still crying, Cici waved at the people as she passed, unable to stop herself from laughing when she recognized the school marching band that Savannah had joined all standing on a mini-platform and pretending to play their instruments in clearly practiced choreography.

It really seemed like the whole town was there as the carriage drew her the short distance. In her head, Cici knew that the song was coming to an end, but it almost seemed like it could never end. Like she was pulled into a different reality where time didn't matter and her whole life could be spent in the brilliance and spectacle of the moment.

But then her ride pulled into the town circle and she saw them, the rest of her siblings, their partners, the Gamals...

...and Baz.

He was wearing a suit, dressed to the absolute nines with his hair perfectly coiffed and his tie her favorite color of royal blue. As she approached, he knelt down, and she could see the little black box in his hand.

It was happening.

It really was happening.

Her carriage finally slowed to a stop and somehow, Papa was there again, hand outstretched to walk her down from it. And he kept a hold of her right hand until she was in front of Baz, the love of her life, where he finally let go and stepped away.

Cici wished she wasn't such a mess. She knew her eyes were

red from crying and could feel that her nose was starting to snot. Her cheeks were a flaming red and she wasn't even wearing her nice clothes!

But it didn't matter. None of it mattered, because Baz, the man she loved, the man she wanted to spend the rest of her life with, was in front of her offering just that.

The final lines of the song rang out, drifting over on the wind like an angelic chorus just for them.

Is it the look in your eyes,

Or is it this dancing juice?

Who cares, baby, I think I wanna marry you!

A truly massive cheer erupted from the gathered crowd as the song drifted out, giving Cici enough time to draw in several greedy gulps of air.

And then it was quiet.

Baz, with ever the sense of dramatic timing, let that silence ring out for several seconds, before speaking.

"Cecilia Miller," he murmured, and it was like his voice was honey itself. She gasped, and as if to echo her, a violin began to softly play nearby. "You've been in my life for many years. From a precocious kid who I helped keep out of trouble or saved from falling out of trees."

"That only happened once!"

"-to an amazing, grown woman who dedicates so much of her life to enriching the lives of everyone around her.

"You've taught me how to love better, how to live better, how to *be* better. You've brought so much joy into my life and given me a direction when I was lost. I am eternally grateful for every second we have together, and I want a million more. A *billion* more.

"I want to spend the rest of my life with you."

"This is amazing," Cici whispered, her voice cracking. The tears were coming in earnest and she could faintly here the click of a camera over the sweet musings of the violin, but none of that mattered. The only thing that mattered was Baz and their love.

"I see so much for us. I see us having children, taking them to whatever sports or drama event they're a part of. I see Christmases under the tree and dozens of summers driving ridiculously far to go berry picking. I see us holding each other during the hard times, and dancing together during the good times.

"I see us growing old together. Growing wiser."

"Me too."

He nodded, and finally popped open that little black box. In it, she saw a truly beautiful ring, simple, yet elegant, with scrolling silver details and only a single, royal blue gem in the center.

"The first step to all of that happening is you saying yes. So, Cecilia Miller, will you do me the honor of being my wife?"

The sob that escaped her throat was full of so much that for a moment she couldn't speak. But when she finally recovered, she drew in a shaky enough breath to say: "I've been waiting for you to ask that."

"I know, my love. So is that a yes?"

"It's the biggest yes you've ever heard!"

Another enormous cheer erupted from the town as Baz slid the ring onto her finger. Cici's hands were shaking, but it slid true, and then suddenly they were hugging and kissing, Baz lifting her up and spinning her around like she always loved.

"I love you!" she heard him cry over the swelling celebration. "I love you, Cecilia Miller!"

"It's gonna be Cecilia Gamal soon," she countered, nearly beside herself with joy. "You better get used to it!"

"I'll have our whole lives to do just that," he said, before kissing her fiercely.

"Oh, and Baz?"

"Yeah?"

"I love you too. More than you could ever know. But I'll spend the rest of my life trying to show you exactly how much."

"That's all I could ever ask for."

Their lips clashed together again, fervent and full of the love they had for each other. Cici couldn't think of a happier way to start the next chapter of her life. Looking around her once they parted, she gazed at his face, the face of his family members, of her family members, and the town around them, all watching with their own expressions of joy and compassion.

She had so much support in her life, so much love, and she was going to do her best to return it tenfold to everyone around her. Just like Baz, she could see their futures stretching out ahead of them, full of more goodness than she could ever deserve but wasn't going to question.

Funny, when she was younger, she wanted to be whisked away to a fantasy world. One with elves and dwarves, sorcerers and prophecies, destinies, quests and swords. But she realized as she kissed Baz yet again, that her happily ever after had been a part of the real world the whole time. Right in front of her, in fact.

She just had to be brave enough to claim it.

HELLO READER! I hope you enjoyed Cecilia and Baz's love story. The next story was a first of its kind for me, but since I wrote this one, I've done several more and readers always love them! I felt like the story wouldn't be complete without giving Papa Miller his own love story. So in the next book, he ends up falling in love with none other than the town librarian. I hope you're ready to give this later in life, second chance at love romance a try!

You can find Montgomery (Papa Miller) and Jeanette's love story on all major retailers. But if you haven't given my bookstore a go yet, I'd love for you to give it a try and support my small author business. Scan the QR code below (might be on the next page, depending on the book format) to be taken to Cowboy Fallin' in Love Again at Natalie Dean Books. If scanning QR codes isn't your thing, you can find my store here: nataliedean books.com Just look under the Miller stories tab for Brides of Miller Ranch, N.M., and you should be able to find this book.

ABOUT THE AUTHOR

Born and raised in a small coastal town in the south, I was raised to treasure family and love the Lord. I'm a dedicated home-schooling mom who loves to travel and spend time with my growing-up-too-fast son.

When I'm not busy writing or running my business, you can find me cleaning house, cooking dinner, feeding our three rescue cats, trying to make learning fun and coaxing my son to pick up his toys. On less busy days, you may also find me paddling down a spring run in Florida, hiking a mountain trail in Georgia (on the rare vacation to the mountains), or enjoying a book.

If you love Natalie Dean books, you can be notified of new releases by signing up to my newsletter at nataliedeanauthor.com, where you will also receive two free short stories for signing up. Just click on the "Free Books" tab at the top and you'll be on your way!

Also, as previously mentioned, I've opened my own online bookstore and I'd love your support! As of June 2024, I'm selling my ebooks at Natalie Dean Books. By late summer or fall 2024, I should have audiobooks, regular paperbacks, large print paperbacks, dyslexic print paperbacks and signed paperbacks all available. At the request of my loyal readers, I'll also be adding merchandise, such as glasses, cups, magnets and more. So come check out my small mom-owned author business at nataliedeanbooks.com.

You can also scan the QR code below to be taken to the home page of Natalie Dean Books.

facebook.com/nataliedeanromance

9 781964 875163